W*illy Mayk*it
in
Space

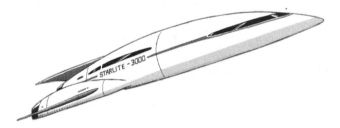

Greg Trine

Illustrations by James Burks

D0106721

HOUGHTON MIFFLIN HARCOURT
Boston   New York

www.hmhco.com

Text set in Dante MT Std

Library of Congress Cataloging-in-Publication Data
Trine, Greg.
Willy Maykit in space / Greg Trine ; illustrations by James Burks.
pages cm
ISBN 978-0-544-31351-4
[1. Outer space—Fiction. 2. Life on other planets—Fiction. 3. School field trips—Fiction. 4. Humorous stories.] I. Burks, James (James R.), illustrator. II. Title.
PZ7.T7356Wil 2015
[Fic]—dc23
2014015882

Manufactured in the United States of America
TK 10 9 8 7 6 5 4 3 2 1
45XXXXXXXX

To Marcos, Anna, and Sara

—G.T.

For Maddie and Max—zing blat blort!

—J.B.

Chapter 1

AROUND THE BEND

When Willy Maykit was three years old, his father went on an African safari and came home with amazing stories of lions, tigers, and bears. Or at least lions, elephants, and hippos. There are no tigers or bears in Africa. But they're doing fine in the elephant and hippo department.

Mr. Maykit was a bigtime scientist and an even bigger-time explorer. "There's a whole world out there, Willy," he often said. "There's always something interesting around the next bend."

Willy didn't know what his father was talking about. He was only three. He thought Bend was the name of a town in Oregon.

The following year, Willy's dad went on an Arctic safari and came home with stories of polar bears, walruses, and icebergs.

Then there was a trip to the Antarctic, followed by more stories, and more talk about what was lurking around the next bend.

One year Mr. Maykit journeyed to the bottom of the ocean and saw sea creatures twenty feet long. He saw giant squids and enormous sharks.

This went on and on, one amazing journey after another, including a trip to Mars, and another to . . . uh . . . Uranus.

And then, when Willy was eight years old, his

father wandered into the Amazon jungle. He was never seen again.

No more amazing stories. No more Mr. Maykit.

Maybe he was swallowed by a giant anaconda, Willy thought. Maybe he fell into a river and was gobbled up by piranhas. Maybe he was captured by headhunters.

Or foothunters.

You never hear about foothunters. They're that sneaky.

What happened to Mr. Maykit? No one knew.

And Willy began to realize what his father had meant when he said there was always something interesting around the next bend. This happened one day when he rounded a corner, which is a lot like rounding a bend, and practically smacked right into Cindy Das. Cindy Das, who just happened to be the prettiest girl in class.

Willy opened his mouth to say, "Excuse me, Cindy." But what came out was "Mumble, mumble, mumble."

So he tried again. He wanted to say something like, "Have a good weekend, Cindy." But what came out was "Mumble, mumble, mumble."

Willy couldn't get his mouth to work properly, not with Cindy standing right there, staring at him with her almost-smile.

Then the almost-smile turned into a full-on

smile. Dimples appeared. Willy kept his mouth shut and stared. If he couldn't talk to her half-smile, he certainly couldn't talk to her dimples.

"You make me laugh, Willy Maykit," she said, and she walked away.

"Dad was right," Willy said to himself. "There really is something interesting around the bend."

It was what his father had been saying all along. There was a whole world out there, waiting to be discovered. And right then, standing on the corner, watching Cindy head down the street, Willy decided it was up to him to pick up where his father had left off. After all, being an explorer was in his blood.

So when Willy heard the news about the class field trip to Planet Ed, he jumped at the chance. He actually stood up from his desk and jumped.

"Is there a problem, Mr. Maykit?" Mr. Jipthorn

asked. Mr. Jipthorn was Willy's teacher. He was also the tallest person Willy had ever seen. Long arms, long legs, long fingers, long underwear. Well, he *probably* had long underwear. Even many of the stories he told were *tall* tales.

"Willy, is there a problem?" he asked again. Students didn't just jump out of their chairs for no reason. Not unless they had to use the bathroom. Or maybe had an ant roaming around in their shorts.

"None at all," said Willy.

"You jumped."

"Just excited about Planet Ed." Willy couldn't help himself. There were probably lots of bends on Planet Ed. There was not only a whole world out there — there was also a whole universe.

But wait a second. Wasn't Planet Ed far away? Very far away? Normally they didn't allow fourth-grade field trips outside the solar system, but some-one had just donated a Starlite 3000 to the school, complete with an android pilot. As you probably know, the Starlite 3000 is the fastest ship in the sky. It's also the safest, and thus the perfect vehicle for fourth-grade field trips.

The problem would be getting permission to go. Mrs. Maykit had lost her adventuring husband. She probably didn't want an adventuring son. She might not understand the concept of things lurking around bends, and that exploring the universe would be even more interesting than exploring the world.

With this thought, Willy sat back down. He really wanted to boldly go where no fourth-grader had gone before, but what if his mom wouldn't let him?

Mr. Jipthorn started passing out permission slips. "Get these signed or you won't be going on the field trip," he said. "And trust me, you don't want to miss *this* trip."

Willy sure didn't. For the rest of the day, he sat at his desk wondering what to do. How could he get his mother to sign the permission slip?

And then, right before the bell rang, it came to him. Today was Friday. Friday was bring-lots-of-paperwork-home-to-have-your-parents-sign day. There were hot-lunch order forms, and recess-monitor forms, forms for the school play, music-lesson sign-up sheets, bake-sale sheets . . . and right in the middle of it all, Willy placed the permission slip for the class field trip to Planet Ed.

It was the best plan he could come up with: Overload his mother with so much information that she wouldn't stop and read the fine print.

Chapter 2
THE BRIBE

After school, Willy raced home. "Hi, Mom," he said, throwing his backpack on the couch. Then he pulled out the stack of papers and placed them on the dining room table.

"How was school?" his mother asked.

"Fine." He pointed to the table. "Got some papers for you to sign."

"Anything interesting?"

Willy yawned. "Boring school stuff." Then he headed to his room, keeping his fingers crossed.

Willy's bedroom was in the attic, because it had the best view in the house. From there he could see the landing strip where his father had landed his plane. He could also see the harbor, in case his father was returning by boat.

Please don't read the fine print, Mom, Willy said to himself as he climbed the spiral staircase to the attic. *I really want to go to Planet Ed.*

Did he ever.

At the top of the stairs, he grabbed a box of Cheerios and opened the attic window. Then he stepped out onto the roof and whistled for Phelps.

Phelps was his pet seagull. Well, not exactly. He was more like a seagull acquaintance. When Willy's father first vanished in the Amazon, Willy often sat on the roof, munching on Cheerios, watching the harbor and the airstrip, and thinking hopeful thoughts.

His father never came, but Phelps did. He knew a sad boy when he saw one. Or at least he noticed the food the boy was eating.

"Caw," the seagull had said, staring at the Cheerios in Willy's hand.

Willy held a handful out to the bird and watched as he pecked away.

They had been hanging out ever since. Willy named him Phelps because he didn't look like a Charlie or a Jack.

So now, with his father long gone, Willy sat on the roof and watched the sky for his favorite bird companion. A few moments later, Phelps flapped down, landed on the roof, and waddled over.

"Caw," he said, looking at the Cheerios in Willy's hand.

"Planet Ed, Phelps," Willy said. "Can you believe it? Planet Ed."

Ed is a strange name for a planet . . . a very strange name. Look at any list of planets and Ed will probably stand out:

SATURN

NEPTUNE

ED

MERCURY

Uh . . . URANUS

Which one doesn't belong? Planet Ed, of course.

Ed was discovered by Ed the Astronomer, who wasn't a real astronomer at all. Most people knew him as Ed the janitor at Mohave Middle School or Ed from the Mohave Bowling Team. He just happened to have an enormous telescope and an eye for things floating around in the night sky looking like undiscovered planets.

One moonless night he was out in his backyard, gazing through his telescope, and there it was: a new planet, just sitting there.

So Ed the janitor named the planet Ed. Did this mean that he had the biggest ego this side of the

Rio Grande? Not exactly. His father's name was Ed. So was his dog's.

Planet Ed . . . It had a nice ring to it.

Phelps wasn't all that interested in exploring other planets. He didn't care about boldly going where no fourth-grader had gone before. He was more of a sit-around-and-eat-anchovies kind of guy. In fact, anchovies were his favorite subject.

Still, Cheerios weren't bad, and Willy was the boy who shared them with him. So Phelps ate his snack and tried to look interested as Willy went on and on about wanting to go to Planet Ed for his class field trip, about being his father's son, and how someone had to be the explorer in the family.

"What do you think, Phelps?" Willy asked. "It's up to me, right?"

"*Caw,*" went Phelps.

"Exactly."

And then, right in the middle of their discussion, Willy heard his mother scream. "Planet Ed!"

"Rats," Willy said. "She read the fine print."

"Willy, get down here!" yelled his mother.

"See you later, Phelps."

"*Caw.*"

Willy climbed back inside and closed the window. Then he looked at himself in the mirror before going downstairs. What he saw was his father's son, the son of an adventurer. Somehow he had to make his mother see it too. He was a Maykit, and Maykits explore the world. And maybe the universe.

"Willy?" his mother called again.

"Coming."

Mrs. Maykit was sitting at the table, permission slip in hand, when Willy got downstairs. Her hair was mussed and her face red. "If you think I'm letting you leave the solar system, you have another think coming."

Willy crossed his fingers and shoved them into his pockets. "It's a school trip, Mom," he said. "It's educational."

His mother didn't say anything, and her face was getting redder by the second.

Willy kept talking. "It's a brand-new Starlite 3000 with an android pilot. They wouldn't let us go if it wasn't safe. Randy Simpkins is going. So is Cindy Das." He didn't know if this was true. But he figured if he kept talking, his mother would get her normal skin color back.

What he didn't mention was his father. He was his father's son—that much was true—but bringing it up would just cause his mother to dig in even deeper. Best to stick to the education argument.

"I'll take lots of pictures, Mom. I'll write a sixty-page report."

Willy's red-faced mother said nothing. She kept

staring at the permission slip. Finally she said, "I'll think about it, Willy."

"I'll think about it" is way better than a no, Willy thought with a smile. *"I'll think about it" is almost a yes.*

"Good idea, Mom. Think about it. Sleep on it. I'll come home in one piece, I promise."

That night Willy couldn't sleep. What would his mom have to say about it in the morning? Maybe having all night to ponder the subject was a bad idea. Thinking about it would just bring back bad memories of his father's disappearance.

Willy needed to stack the deck in his favor. He needed a bribe. And what's the best bribe in the world besides diamonds? Breakfast in bed, of course. The trick was to make the breakfast without waking his mother. It had to be a complete surprise, so she'd say something like, "Wow, this is almost as good as diamonds. Of course you can travel to another solar system, you dear boy."

And so, early the next morning, when it was still dark out, Willy descended the spiral staircase and tiptoed to the kitchen. Then he got busy making bacon, eggs, and toast. When it was finished, he carried it to his mother's bedroom and woke her up.

"What's all this?" she said with a small yawn.

"A gift from a son who loves you?" Willy didn't mean for it to sound like a question. And, to be

honest, it wasn't the best breakfast in the world, but what it lacked in flavor, Willy made up for in service. He refilled the juice glass. He even spread jam on the toast.

Then he sat on the edge of the bed. "Anything else I can get for you, Mom? Sorry, I didn't know how to make coffee."

"This juice is perfect." She took a sip. Then she looked up at him and said, "You will be careful, won't you, Willy?"

Somewhere inside his heart, a band began to play. Willy jumped off the bed and danced right there in his mother's bedroom. It was the I'm-heading-out-of-the-solar-system-thank-you-very-much dance.

"Thanks, Mom. I promise I'll be careful." Then he danced some more.

The bribe had worked. Willy Maykit was going to Planet Ed!

Chapter 3
THE STARLITE 3000

The thing about androids is that they won't get your jokes. They don't have a humorous bone in their body. They might not even have bones. But this did not keep Willy from trying. On the day of the field trip, he walked up to the pilot—an android named Max—who was outside the airship, kicking the tires and doing other important safety checks.

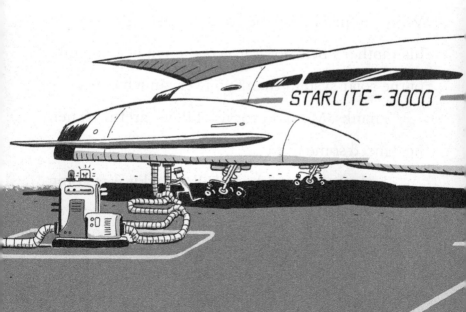

"Knock, knock," Willy said.

Max looked up. "I beg your pardon?" Max might have been an android, but he looked a lot like Willy's uncle Ralph. Same black hair, same gigantic eyebrows.

"Knock, knock," Willy said again.

The android blinked.

"You're supposed to say, 'Who's there?'"

"Who's there?"

"Boo," Willy said.

"Hello, Boo. I'm Max."

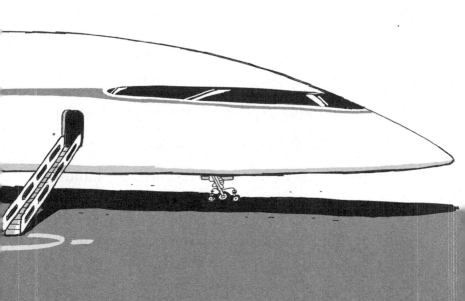

"No, you're supposed to say, 'Boo who?'"

"Boo who?"

Willy grinned. "Why are you crying?"

Max blinked a few more times, but he didn't laugh. Willy would have to try harder.

But he would try harder later. Right now he had to board the ship.

The field trip to Planet Ed would not be an overnighter—they'd be back on Earth by four o'clock—but Mr. Jipthorn allowed everyone to bring some sort of carry-on. For most of the kids in Willy's class, this was their school backpack. Willy brought his father's duffel. It was bigger—it could hold more stuff. Plus, it belonged to his father—his father the famous explorer. If it was good enough for Mr. Maykit, it was good enough for Willy.

Willy waved to his mother, who was standing in the school parking lot with the other parents. Then he climbed aboard and found a seat near a window and looked out at her. *Don't worry, Mom,* he mouthed. *See you soon.*

Mrs. Maykit nodded, but a single tear made its way down her cheek. She walked over to the ship and kicked a tire. Sometimes kicking things makes you feel better. This seemed to be the case with Mrs. Maykit. She wiped away the tear and looked up at Willy. *I love you,* she mouthed. Then she stepped back, and the ship lifted into the air.

It was just after six in the morning when the Starlite 3000 left the earth's atmosphere.

There's not much to look at when you're traveling along at many times the speed of light. Everything is streaked and blurred. Willy wondered why the Starlite 3000 had windows at all. It wasn't as if he could gaze through the glass and say, "Now *there's* an attractive planet," or "Check out that interesting asteroid."

There were probably plenty of attractive planets out there, and lots of interesting asteroids. But Willy couldn't see them. It was just one big blur. So he turned away from the window and reached into his sweatshirt pocket for a handful of Cheerios.

"Cheerios?" Randy Simpkins, who was sitting beside Willy, looked up from his electronic book.

"Breakfast of champions," Willy said.

"Wrong cereal." Randy turned back to his book and tapped it to flip the page.

"How about they taste good?"

"That'll work."

"Want to go explore the ship?" Willy asked.

Randy held up his book. "Just getting to the good part. But I'd like a full report." Randy was big on full reports. "Take good notes."

"I'll think about it." Willy wasn't sure if there were bends inside the Starlite 3000, but there were probably plenty of nooks and crannies. It was a very big ship — it had many rooms.

Willy unzipped his duffel, which was at his feet, and threw in the Cheerios. "Hands off my bag," he said to Randy. Then he wandered down the main aisle into a room where a bunch of girls were seated around a table. One of them was Cindy Das. Willy wanted to say something like "Good morning" or "Whatcha doing?" but with Cindy Das sitting there with her almost-smile, all that came out was "Mumble, mumble, mumble."

He moved on to the movie room, where they were showing a film he'd seen before. The next room had a Ping-Pong table. And the next was some sort of library with lots of computer screens. Mr. Jipthorn was sitting at one of the computers.

"Willy?" Mr. Jipthorn said, giving him one of his teacher looks.

"Just exploring the ship," Willy told him.

"I'd like a full report," Mr. Jipthorn said.

Oh, no! Willy cringed. To Mr. Jipthorn, a full report meant perfect penmanship and even more perfect grammar. It meant all sorts of nasty things, like hard work and . . . *effort.*

Willy kept walking, opening and closing cupboards and closet doors. He checked out all six bathrooms. The Starlite 3000 was packed with stuff.

With any luck, Mr. Jipthorn would forget about the full report he'd requested. Hopefully.

Finally, Willy headed up front and sat in the copilot's seat next to Max. There is something very wrong about a fourth-grader sitting in the copilot's chair when a spaceship is traveling along at many times the speed of light, but if it was okay with Max, it was okay with Willy Maykit.

"Knock, knock," Willy said.

"I beg your pardon?"

Willy gave him a look. "You forgot already? We've been through this."

"Oh, who's there?"

"Oink-oink."

"Oink-oink who?" asked the pilot.

"Make up your mind. Are you a pig or an owl?"

Max blinked a few times. He didn't laugh.

Willy tried again.

"Knock, knock."

"Who's there?"

"Doris."

"Doris who?"

"Doris locked. That's why I'm knocking."

It was no use. Max wouldn't know a joke if it bit him in the microchip.

Willy stayed in the copilot's chair for the rest of the trip. Max didn't mind. He didn't understand any of Willy's jokes, but he seemed to like the company.

Somewhere around Pluto, Willy stopped trying

to make Max laugh and gave his attention to the instrument panel in front of him.

There were green buttons and red buttons. Knobs and levers and—

"What's that?" Willy asked.

"We call it the steering wheel."

"Aren't you supposed to be hanging on to it?"

The android shook his head. "We're going much too fast to steer."

"Autopilot?" Willy asked.

"Something like that."

A few hours later, they were orbiting Planet Ed. "Now *there's* an attractive planet," Willy said. It looked a lot like Earth. It was round, anyway. And there were oceans and huge areas of land.

Max grabbed the steering wheel and directed the ship closer to the surface.

"Are you sure this is Planet Ed?" Willy asked as they prepared to land.

"What do you mean?"

Willy pointed. There were trees and rivers and mountains. "It looks a lot like Colorado."

"It's Planet Ed," Max said. "Trust me."

Willy did trust him—but it still looked like Colorado.

Chapter 4

PLANET ED

The ship landed in a clearing in what looked like a huge forest, or, as Willy called it, Colorado, though he knew this was not the case. You can't travel through space at many times the speed of light and end up in the Rockies. Can you?

Willy looked out the window at the trees and the mountains, beyond which there were dark clouds. *Storm clouds,* Willy thought, *and me without my rain boots.* Not to mention his umbrella.

But the storm clouds were miles away. Willy had a whole planet to explore. He'd worry about the weather later.

Mr. Jipthorn pushed open the door of the ship and stepped out, followed by the entire class. "Boys and girls, let me have your attention," Mr. Jipthorn began. "We are leaving here in three hours. Feel free to look around, but do not wander off alone."

"Planet Ed," Willy said to Randy. "Can you believe it?"

"Not really," Randy said. He held out his arm. "Pinch me."

"If you say so." Willy was an expert pincher.

"Ouch!" Randy said, but he was smiling. "Wow. Planet Ed."

"See you later, Randy."

"Where are you going?"

"Exploring. It's what I do." Willy dragged his duffel away from the other kids, completely ignoring the teacher's instructions.

Mr. Jipthorn was going on and on about staying nearby, about safety on a foreign planet, about keeping close to the ship. And everyone was listening.

Everyone except Willy Maykit.

He was too busy hauling his duffel

to the edge of the clearing and yanking on the zip-per. Seconds later, Phelps poked his head out.

"*Caw,*" Phelps said.

Willy knew this was the bird's way of saying, "I don't appreciate being cooped up for three hours, but thanks for the Cheerios."

"You're welcome," Willy muttered.

Phelps took to the air.

Willy followed his bird into the forest, run-ning along what looked like a hiking trail. "Phelps, wait up."

"*Caw.*" Phelps flew on, a hundred yards ahead, then two hundred.

After a while Willy stopped running. No way could he keep up with a bird. Instead, he took his time, exploring the woods along the trail. When-ever the path wrapped around a huge boulder on the right or suddenly jogged to the left, Willy caught his breath. Hadn't his father always told him there could be something interesting around the next bend?

Willy kept walking, and as he walked, he whistled. It was a tune he'd learned from his father. If it was good enough for Mr. Maykit, it was good enough for Willy.

He wandered deeper and deeper into the forest. Now and then he thought of turning back, but each time he did, the trail bent, and Willy had to see what was beyond it.

He was so caught up in the hike and paying attention to what was happening on the ground that he didn't notice what was happening overhead. He didn't see the dark clouds moving in.

Not until a shadow passed over him. Not until it started to rain.

It came lightly at first. Willy barely felt it. And then it picked up a tad.

Only it was much more than a tad. It was the

downpour to beat all downpours. The water not only came down in sheets, it came down in blankets. Pretty strange. But this is a different planet we're talking about. It was raining harder than he'd ever seen it. Willy ran to the nearest tree for shelter. That helped a little, but not much. Soon the wind picked up, and rain came at him sideways.

And then —

CRACK!

Lightning struck. Hanging out under a tree might not be the best idea, Willy realized. Didn't lightning strike the high places? And weren't trees rather . . . high?

Willy shoved himself away from the tree and ran along the path. Only there was no longer a path. It had been washed away.

Which way back to the ship? Willy could only guess. He pointed himself in what he thought was the right direction and ran.

CRACK!

This time it wasn't lightning. A large tree branch fell beside him.

CRACK!

Then another. It was bad enough getting drenched, but now trees were dropping their body parts on him.

CRACK!

More lightning.

CRACK!

And tree branches.

Up ahead he spotted two cabin-size boulders lying next to each other with a triangle of dry space beneath. Willy ran for it and crawled in just as the rain turned to hail. Hail the size of golf balls pounded all around him.

One hailstone was a bit larger. Make that a lot larger. And it had wings.

Wait a minute. That was no hailstone. It was

Phelps, flapping down out of the storm. He landed in front of Willy and said, *"Caw,"* which was probably the bird's way of saying, "Move over, big guy, and pass the Cheerios."

Willy moved over, and Phelps crawled in beside him. The two of them watched the storm rage on. Lightning flashed; tree branches fell. It was a long time before the hail turned back to rain.

Willy stayed under the protection of the boulders until it stopped. Then he crawled out and got to his feet. He had no idea what time it was, but it seemed like he'd been under the boulders for ages. "Hmm," Willy said. "Time flies even when you're *not* having fun. Back to the ship, Phelps. Follow me."

"Caw," said Phelps as he took to the air.

If there was no sign of the trail before the hailstorm, there was certainly no sign of it now. Willy stepped over and around the fallen tree branches and kept moving in what he thought was the right direction. The miles clicked by.

He shivered from the cold. "Climb inside the ship and turn on the heat—that's the ticket," he said to himself. "Dry out, watch a movie, and head back to good ol' planet Earth."

That was the plan, anyway.

But when he pushed through the trees into the clearing, there was no ship. No classmates. No Mr. Jipthorn. Willy spun around. Obviously this was the wrong clearing. He started back the way he'd come, wondering where he'd taken a wrong turn. And that's when he spotted his duffel, lying where he'd left it after releasing Phelps. It was the right clearing after all.

But where was the ship? Willy scanned the sky above. Nothing but dark clouds.

And no sign of the Starlite 3000.

Chapter 5
ALONE

"Really?" Willy looked up and searched from one end of the sky to the other. "Are you kidding me?"

Being stranded on another planet had to be one of the worst things that could ever happen to a person. Worse than being picked last in kickball. Worse than being force-fed Brussels sprouts. Worse than—

Well, let's just say it was worse than a lot of

things. You name it. Being stranded on a distant planet had to be worse.

Willy stood in the middle of the clearing. He thought of his tearful mother, standing in the school parking lot, and his last words to her: *See you soon.* See you soon? Not likely. Not without a spaceship to get him home.

"Sorry, Mom," he muttered.

He scanned the sky above. Sooner or later someone would see that he was missing. The ship would turn around and pick him up. "Any second now," he said out loud. He looked up at the sky again.

But "any second now" came and went. So did any minute now. Willy was confused. How could they have left without him? Wasn't it the teacher's job to make sure everyone was on board?

It was the teacher's job, all right. But Mr. Jipthorn wasn't exactly in his right mind.

• • • •

As you probably remember, the rain had not only come down in sheets, it had come down in blankets. The wind blew; lightning cracked.

So did the branches. Trees were dropping their body parts all over the place. One of these body parts—a rather large one, in fact—landed on Mr. Jipthorn's head, and down he went, unconscious.

Max the pilot, who looked a lot like Willy's uncle Ralph but was in fact an android and had android strength, picked up Mr. Jipthorn and carried him onto the ship. The kids followed. Outside, the storm raged on.

CRACK!

More tree limbs.

CRACK!

And lightning strikes.

"We've got to get out of here," Max said as he fired up the Starlite 3000. "Is everyone on board?"

"Yes!" the kids yelled. They were too scared to

really check. The lightning was getting closer, and now they could hear hail—golf-ball size, with a few watermelon-size ones thrown in—smacking the ship. "Get us out of here, Max!"

And so Max did. The Starlite lifted off the ground and rocketed away.

Willy kept glancing up at the sky. "Really?" he kept saying.

After a while he walked over to his duffel, unzipped it, and pulled out his jacket. Besides Phelps, he had packed only two other items, his jacket and a joke book. He had really wanted to make Max laugh. When he ran out of jokes he knew by memory, the book would give him plenty more.

Now he didn't care if he made anyone laugh. He was stranded on a faraway planet, in a faraway solar system. Laughing was the last thing on his mind.

He flipped open the book to a random page and

read out loud. "What's black and white and read all over? A newspaper."

Nope, Willy wasn't in a laughing mood.

He closed the book and sat down on his duffel, which wasn't exactly dry, but at least it wasn't muddy. Then he watched the sky. The clouds were starting to clear, but there was no sign of the ship. He wondered how cold it got at night on Planet Ed. And what about food and water?

Panic grabbed him. What if his classmates didn't figure it out? What if they didn't realize he was missing? What if he really was stranded? What if—

Willy heard something.

"Willy Maykit, where are you?"

Someone, or some*thing,* was calling his name. He hadn't given much thought to the creatures of Planet Ed, but apparently they knew his name.

"Willy Maykit."

There it was again. Willy got to his feet and grabbed one of the fallen branches. He cocked it back like a baseball bat, ready to swing.

"Willy."

The voice was getting closer. Whatever came through those trees was in trouble. Willy would swing first and ask questions later.

But what if the creatures of Planet Ed were enormous? Clonking this one with a tree branch probably wouldn't help much. Willy glanced at the branch in his hand. It was all he had to work with.

The voice came again. "Willy, are you there?"

Willy kept his mouth shut. If it *was* an enormous creature, he'd have to swing plenty hard to bring it down. He crouched, tree branch cocked and ready.

And then—

The creature came crashing through the bushes into the clearing.

Only it wasn't a creature. And it certainly wasn't enormous. In fact, it was someone Willy recognized.

"Cindy Das! What are you doing here?" Willy was so shocked at seeing her that he forgot to say "Mumble, mumble, mumble."

Even Cindy noticed. "Wow, you can speak in full sentences."

"What are you doing here?" Willy asked again.

"I saw you weren't on the ship, so I went looking for you." Her almost-smile appeared. "I slipped out the back door."

"Thanks, I guess." Willy spun around, gesturing to the emptiness of the clearing. "See anything missing?"

Cindy nodded. "I didn't think they'd leave without us."

"Me neither."

Chapter 6

NOT ALONE

But at least now he wasn't alone. Willy pointed to his duffel. "Have a seat, Cindy. It's hardly muddy at all."

Cindy sat down, and Willy joined her.

"What do we do now?" she asked.

"Good question."

The two of them sat and watched the sky. Willy felt a little less afraid now that he wasn't alone. Misery loves company. So do people stranded on faraway planets.

They kept scanning for the Starlite 3000. Still no sign of it. Meanwhile, the sun was getting lower and lower in the sky.

"They'll figure it out," Cindy said after a while. "They'll be here any minute. I'm almost sure of it."

Almost? Willy gave her a look and saw that her almost-smile had vanished. Cindy Das was never without her almost-smile.

The sun went down, and out came a couple of moons, one white and one orange. They gave them just enough light to see. Just enough light to see that no one was coming to their rescue.

"Any ideas?" Cindy asked.

Willy shrugged. "Sleep?"

The ground was still soggy, but it was a little drier beneath one of the trees where there was a bed of pine needles (or the Planet Ed version of pine needles), and soon they had a comfy place to lie down.

Willy was about to doze off when Cindy asked, "Why'd you do it, Willy?"

"Why'd I do what?"

"Why did you wander off? Didn't you hear Mr. Jipthorn tell us not to?"

Willy gazed up at the two moons, thinking of his father. "Exploring is in my blood. I couldn't help but wander off."

Cindy nodded like she understood.

They were quiet for a while, listening to the wind through the trees and to the Planet Ed version of crickets. Willy stared up at the stars. "Night, Dad," he whispered.

Willy's father was a little too far away to hear his son's whispers. As you know, he had vanished into the Amazon jungle a year earlier. Here's the good news: He wasn't dead. His heart was beating as strong as ever.

But he wasn't exactly safe, either.

A year before, he had been examining what he thought was a new form of orchid and getting rather excited. He was a scientist. Scientists are always getting excited over strange things.

Would you get excited over a flower? Didn't think so.

But Mr. Maykit sure was. He was looking at the orchid when he noticed a set of eyes staring back at him. Make that many sets of eyes.

These were the foothunters. They're so sneaky, no one's ever heard of them.

They grabbed Willy's father and dragged him back to their camp, which took three days. He'd been locked up ever since.

It was a very scary place. Everyone wore shrunken feet around their necks.

And they kept staring at Mr. Maykit's feet.

• • • •

Willy had no idea when he nodded off. He only knew that something caused him to wake up. Was it a sound? A twig snap? The low growl of a Planet Ed creature of the night?

Willy wasn't sure. He rolled over and came face-to-face with a set of eyes staring down at him. The eyes belonged to what looked like a boy about Willy's age, only not a human boy. Even in the moonlight, Willy could see that his skin was a greenish color and he had two antennae coming out of his head.

"Let me guess," the alien boy said. "Left behind on a school field trip?"

Willy got to his feet. "Uh . . . what?" he asked, rubbing his eyes. Maybe he was dreaming. He was on a foreign planet. It made sense that he'd dream about aliens.

"Field trip?" the boy said. "Left behind?"

Willy kept blinking and rubbing his eyes.

Finally, Cindy, who was now standing, spoke up. "Yes, we were left behind on a school field trip."

"Welcome to the club," the boy said. "I'm Norp. I was left behind on my school field trip a week ago."

"I'm Willy," Willy said, finding his voice.

"Cindy," Cindy said.

Norp nodded. Then he lowered his voice. "You can't stay here."

"Why not?" Cindy asked.

The boy gestured to the clearing. "You're in the

open, and it's night. Nighttime is when the monsters come out."

Willy and Cindy exchanged a glance. "Monsters?" they said together.

"Yes, monsters. Don't you have monsters on your planet?"

"Of course," Willy said. "I'm pretty sure one's been living under my bed for years."

"There's one in my closet," Cindy added.

"That's where they live on my planet too," Norp said. "Here they roam about in the forest. And they're always hungry." He looked nervously at the trees. "You two better follow me. We don't have much time."

Willy hesitated. All his life he'd been told not to talk to strangers. This guy was not only a stranger, he wasn't even human. And he wanted them to follow him into a deep, dark forest in the middle of the night on a faraway planet?

"Uh . . ." Willy said, not knowing what to do. He glanced at Cindy, but all she could say was, "Uh . . ." Obviously, she'd received the same advice about talking to strangers.

"Monsters," the alien boy said. "I'm not kidding. We have to get out of here."

Willy didn't know what to do. Don't talk to strangers was the rule, and a nonhuman kid was definitely a stranger.

Before he could decide, something went *bump* in the night. Or *smash* and *crunch,* to be exact. Something huge was coming at them through the trees.

"Too late," Norp said. "Here they come."

Chapter 7

MR. JIPTHORN

The kids from Willy's class were still pretty upset from getting caught in a storm with watermelon-size hailstones and seeing Mr. Jipthorn get clonked by a tree branch. Inside the Starlite 3000, many of the kids were crying and wringing their hands, looking at their unconscious teacher and saying things like, "Is he alive?"

"Is he breathing?"

"Is there money in his wallet?"

He was alive. He was breathing. He did have money in his wallet. But he didn't regain consciousness for hours, not until they were almost back to Earth.

Mr. Jipthorn sat up, holding his head. "What happened?" he said.

"Huge storm on Planet Ed," one kid said.

"Hail as big as watermelons," said another. "By the way, how's yours?"

"Pardon me?" Mr. Jipthorn asked.

"How's your melon?"

Mr. Jipthorn kept holding his head and wincing from the pain. "I remember the storm, but what happened?"

"You were hit by a tree branch," Randy said, speaking up. "Max is getting us home. He's really strong. He carried you all by himself."

Mr. Jipthorn nodded and began counting heads. Twenty-eight students, he said to himself. But wait a minute—didn't thirty kids sign up for the field trip? "Who's missing?" he said. "Randy, go check the bathrooms."

Randy did and came back shaking his head.

It took them a while, but they finally figured it out: Willy Maykit and Cindy Das were not on board.

Mr. Jipthorn ran to the cockpit. "Turn this thing around," he said to the pilot.

"No can do." Max pointed to one of the gauges on the control panel. "We're low on fuel."

By now they were in orbit around the earth. Since they were so close and so low on fuel, there was nothing to do but drop the kids off and refuel.

The rescue would have to wait.

Max landed the Starlite 3000 in the school parking lot, and all the kids rushed out. Some of them burst into tears at the sight of their parents. It had been a difficult day, what with being pelted with oversize hail and seeing their teacher get clonked.

Mr. Jipthorn came out last, holding his head.

The parents packed up their kids and drove away, leaving only Mrs. Maykit and Mrs. Das in the parking lot.

While Max wandered around the ship, kicking the tires and doing other important safety checks, Mr. Jipthorn went over to the waiting moms.

"Where's Willy?" said Mrs. Maykit.

"Where's Cindy?" said Mrs. Das.

It wasn't easy getting fuel for the Starlite 3000. It was dark before Max, the android pilot, was able to fire up the ship and head back to Planet Ed.

Mr. Jipthorn didn't come along. He was too busy getting his head stitched back together. "You're a lucky man," one of the doctors told him. "That android may have saved your life."

"Good ol' Max," Mr. Jipthorn muttered to himself.

Chapter 8

SOMETHING BIG AND HAIRY THIS WAY COMES

Norp's antennae twitched. His green skin turned white. "Should have run when we had the chance," he said.

Whatever it was got closer. Twigs and branches snapped. Trees swayed as if they were being shoved aside by something enormous. Then came the roar—like a *T. rex* and a grizzly bear combined, with a hint of killer whale.

Should have followed the nonhuman into the deep, dark forest, Willy thought. He tried to turn and run, but his feet felt like they were nailed to the ground. Something rattled. "What's that?"

"My knees," Cindy said. She couldn't move her feet either, but her knees were working double-time.

Another roar. Much closer this time.

Seconds later, the creature crashed through the trees into the clearing. It was like Bigfoot on steroids—hairy, with huge teeth and claws.

And it was . . . smiling? But it wasn't a friendly smile at all. Maybe it was what Planet Ed creatures of the night did when they were about to have a midnight snack, even though it was probably way past midnight. The point is, this creature looked hungry, and Willy and Cindy were on the menu. And probably Norp, for that matter.

The creature took a step forward, then another, licking its lips.

Willy still couldn't move his legs. Cindy's knees knocked even louder.

And then—

Something fell from the sky, something white and gooey, that went *GLOP* right in the monster's eyes.

Wings flapped overhead. *"Caw!"* Phelps's aim was perfect.

He came back for another pass.

GLOP!

"Nice shot, Phelps!" Willy yelled.

The monster put his paws to his face, crying out in pain. He was probably also pretty grossed out. After all, someone had just pooped in his face.

The monster was blinded, but only temporarily. Now was their chance.

"Run!" Norp yelled. "Follow me."

Willy forced his legs to move, Cindy's knees stopped knocking, and they followed Norp into the deep, dark forest on the faraway planet. It was much better than sticking around to become a monster's midnight snack. They ran deeper into the forest. Deeper into who-knows-what, who-knows-where, with who-knows-who.

Willy fell down several times, over roots and fallen branches — sometimes over nothing. It's hard to stay upright when a monster is hot on your heels. Was the monster hot on his heels? Willy wasn't sure, but that didn't keep him from falling.

"Where are you taking us?" Willy asked, gasping for breath and picking himself up off the ground for the hundredth time.

"A safe place. Trust me," said the alien boy. His antennae were still twitching.

Willy wasn't sure if he could trust a guy with twitching antennae. But twitching antennae had to be better than being munched on.

They kept running. After a while, they came to the edge of a deep canyon above a roaring river.

"Now what?" Cindy asked.

Norp grabbed a vine hanging from a tree. "We swing across, Thortock-style."

"Thortock?" Willy made a face. "Don't you mean Tarzan?"

"I mean Thortock."

"Guy in a loincloth? Runs around in the jungle? Yells a lot?" Willy asked.

"That's him."

"Well, on our planet he's called Tarzan."

Norp placed a vine in Cindy's hand. Then he handed one to Willy. "Okay, Tarzan-style, then. You have your jungle hero and I have mine." Then he launched himself across the canyon. He even added a little alien Thortock yell.

Willy and Cindy followed, landing in a heap on the other side.

"We're not there yet," Norp said. He led Willy and Cindy through a circle of trees growing so close together that they had to turn sideways to slip between them. It was some kind of natural fort. At the center was an enormous tree, ten feet in diameter, maybe more.

"Up we go," Norp said, starting to climb.

Willy and Cindy followed. Could the monsters of Planet Ed swing on vines, Tarzan-style? Or in the Thortock manner? Best to climb the tree and get out of sight, just in case.

The surface of the tree was bumpy, with lots of knots and knobs to cling to and stand on. About ten feet off the ground, they reached the first branches, which spread apart, creating a bowl big enough for two humans and an alien to stretch out in.

Far away in the distance, they could hear the creature roar.

"We're safe," Norp said. "The monsters on this planet can't swing like Thortock. And they can't climb trees."

"Thank goodness," Cindy said.

Willy wasn't so sure. Norp had been there only a week. How did he know what the monsters were capable of? Willy looked out through the branches of the tree. From someplace off in the distance, he heard a roar. Then another.

"How many monsters are there?" Willy asked.

"Not sure," Norp said. "Dozens, maybe."

"Dozens?" Cindy gasped.

"Maybe," Norp said. "But they're out there and we're here. You really can relax. I know what I'm talking about. We're completely safe."

Willy turned around and faced hm. "I'm trying to believe you," he said. "It's not easy."

Norp nodded and gestured for Willy to sit. When he did, Norp leaned forward. "So you two were left behind, huh?"

Willy nodded. "Don't get me started."

"It's a long story," Cindy said.

Norp grinned. "My favorite kind."

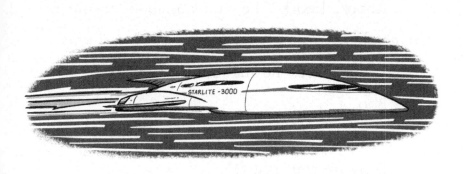

Chapter 9
MAX TO THE RESCUE

As you know, there's not a whole lot to look at when you're traveling along at many times the speed of light. It's not as if you can say, "Now *there's* an attractive planet," or "Check out that interesting asteroid." As you also know, there are probably plenty of attractive planets out there, and more than a few interesting asteroids. But since Max couldn't see any of them, and since he had a three-hour journey ahead of him, he sat back and relaxed, thinking of the boy who had tried to make him laugh.

"Knock, knock," he said out loud, trying to remember.

"Who's there?" he answered himself.

"Boo."

"Boo who?"

"Why are you crying?"

Max didn't get it. Androids aren't exactly wired for humor. He gazed out the window at the streaked universe shooting past. Nothing to see there. Again his thoughts turned to Willy Maykit.

"Knock, knock," he said

"Who's there?"

"Doris."

"Doris who?"

"Door is locked. That's why I'm knocking."

Nothing. Not even a smirk.

The Starlite 3000 raced on through the blurriness of space. Max was determined to figure out what Willy had been getting at. Why did humans spend so much time laughing? He didn't understand. And so, hours later, just as he began his orbit of Planet Ed, he tried again.

"Knock, knock."

"Who's there?"

"Oink-oink."

"Oink-oink who?"

"Make up your mind. Are you a pig or an owl?"

A pig or an owl. Max scratched his chin. He still didn't understand.

He grabbed the steering wheel and directed the ship closer to Planet Ed. *A pig or an owl,* he thought. *A pig or an owl.*

And right then, Max the android pilot smiled. Microchips flashed inside his head—kind of like blowing a fuse, only he didn't have any fuses to blow. He was a microchip kind of android. But something was happening.

His smile got bigger. "A pig or an owl," he said out loud. "A pig or an owl. That's a real knee slapper."

Max couldn't hold it in any longer. He tilted his head back, opened his mouth, and—

"*Ha, ha, ha, ha, ha, ha, ha, ha!*" There was no stopping him. It was the funniest thing he'd ever heard. "*Ha, ha, ha, ha, ha, ha, ha, ha, ha!*"

More microchips flashed. Sparks shot out of his ears. His eyes wobbled in their sockets. "*Ha, ha, ha, ha, ha, ha, ha, ha, ha, ha, ha, ha!*"

The more he laughed, the more he lost control. The microchips inside his body were so busy flashing and throwing off sparks that Max couldn't make his hands and arms do what he wanted.

And Planet Ed was coming up fast!

"Oh, no!" Max said as he continued to laugh. *"Ha, ha, ha.* I can't control the ship. *Ha, ha, ha.* Looks like I'm about to crash into that mountainside. *Ha, ha, ha.*

"*Ha, ha, ha, ha, ha, ha, ha, ha, ha, ha, ha, ha, ha, ha, ha, ha!"*

KABOOM!

It was the biggest fireball ever seen on Planet Ed.

"What was that?"

Willy was right in the middle of his story about getting caught in the rainstorm, about trees dropping their body parts, about hail the size of golf balls—and a few as big as watermelons—when an explosion ripped the night air.

Through the branches of the tree, the sky lit up like the Fourth of July.

Cindy shook her head. "If those monsters have dynamite, that is so unfair."

They kept quiet, listening for more explosions. None came, and they couldn't exactly go investigate. It was too dark, and there were hungry monsters lurking about.

After a while, sleep got the better of them, and they drifted off.

Willy woke up only once during the night, when Phelps landed lightly beside him. If it hadn't been for his favorite bird companion, the Planet Ed creatures of the night might have gobbled him up. "Thanks, Phelps," Willy whispered. "You're the coolest seagull in the universe."

"*Caw*," Phelps replied. Then the two of them drifted off to sleep.

By the way, seagulls snore. Who knew?

Chapter 10
THREE'S COMPANY

The next morning, Willy woke up to a pair of alien eyes staring back at him. "Are you two hungry?" Norp said. "I mean, do Earthlings eat?"

"Of course we eat," Willy said. "And yes, I'm hungry."

"What's for breakfast?" Cindy said, rubbing her eyes.

"I know of a place," Norp said. "Follow me."

Willy glanced at Cindy and shrugged. They didn't know Norp at all, but if he was an evil alien, he wouldn't have shown them his hideout. Hadn't he saved their lives last night?

And so, once again, Willy found himself following a stranger into a deep, dark forest on a faraway planet. Or at least a deep forest—it was no longer dark.

Grrrrrrrrrrrrr!

Norp stopped, antennae twitching. "What was that?"

"My stomach," Willy said. "Don't hungry stomachs growl on your planet?"

"Never," Norp said.

They swung across the canyon like Thortock and a couple of Tarzans and headed through the trees.

"Are you sure the monsters aren't out in the daytime?" Cindy asked.

"Positive," Norp said. "As long as it's light out, we're safe. I think it's too bright for them." He thought for a second. "Of course, I haven't explored the whole planet. The monsters in *this* area don't like the light."

They kept walking, crossed a few creeks, then headed down a slope. After a while, it leveled off into some kind of grove with a very different sort of tree. The leaves on the trees were a light shade of pink—even the tree trunks were pink—and they were filled with apple-size purple fruit. Norp pulled one off a low-hanging branch and took a bite.

Willy and Cindy hesitated. "Are you sure they're edible?" Cindy asked.

Norp grinned, purple juice running down his chin. "Been eating them for a week and I'm still here."

"Yeah, but he's an alien," Cindy whispered.

"I know," Willy whispered back.

"Maybe aliens can handle poison."

"I know."

"What are you two whispering about?" Norp asked. "Isn't telling secrets considered rude on your planet? Come on. Breakfast is served."

"Uh . . ." Willy muttered.

Before he could decide, wings flapped overhead. *"Caw."* Phelps landed beside him. Then he waddled over to a fallen piece of fruit and pecked at it.

If it was good enough for the coolest seagull in the universe, it was good enough for Willy Maykit. "Come on, Cindy," he said. "Let's eat."

Willy and Cindy joined in. "Not bad," Willy said, finishing one piece of fruit and reaching for another. It was much more than not bad. It was the best fruit he'd ever tasted—a combination of apple, orange, and pomegranate rolled into one.

"Not bad at all," Cindy added.

For every piece of fruit Willy ate, Norp ate three. He was a purple-fruit-eating machine.

"We should save some for later," Willy said, "so we don't have to come back here."

And that's when he remembered his duffel. He'd left it in the clearing the night before when the monster chased them off. Everyone agreed that Willy's duffel would be the perfect purple-fruit container.

Willy raced back to the clearing and grabbed the bag. When he returned to the grove of pink trees, Cindy and Norp were already busy picking the purple fruit. Willy joined in and helped them fill the duffel. But hauling a full bag of fruit back to their tree was no easy task. And swinging Tarzan-style while carrying a heavy load proved impossible.

"Now what?" Cindy said, gazing across the canyon.

Willy shrugged. "I may be Tarzan, but I'm no King Kong."

In the end, they dumped the bag of fruit at the edge of the canyon. Then Willy swung across with the empty duffel and held it open as Cindy and Norp tossed the fruit across. The process took most of the day, since they couldn't climb a tree with a full bag either.

"A few at a time," Willy said. "It's the only way."

By the time they got the fruit up into the tree, they were two very tired humans and one exhausted alien.

Fortunately, their tree hideout was big enough for the three of them and a large duffel full of fruit. They were safe from the Planet Ed creatures of the night, and they had plenty to eat. Not bad.

"Now if we can just find a way home," Willy said.

"Someone will come to our rescue," Cindy said cheerfully.

"I don't know." Willy gestured to their alien companion. "Norp's been here a week."

Norp stretched out, lacing his fingers behind his head. "A week at least. I'm starting to lose count of the days."

"And he's still stranded, Cindy," Willy said.

"Earth's only three hours away," Cindy said. "How hard could it be to send a rescue team? It's not rocket science."

"Hmm . . ." Willy said. "Traveling to another solar system at many times the speed of light? I think that *is* rocket science."

"Yeah," Norp said. "If that's not rocket science, I don't know what is."

"You know what I mean," Cindy said. "As soon as they got back to Earth, they should have seen we were missing." She glanced at Norp. "How far is it to your planet?"

"Five days," Norp said. When Willy's and Cindy's

mouths dropped open, he added, "They believe in long field trips on my planet."

"So it might be a while before they get back here," Willy said.

Norp sat up. "You mean *if* they get back here." He reached into the duffel and grabbed a few of the purple fruit. "Dinner, anyone?"

Willy took a couple and handed one to Cindy. They ate in silence. It still tasted good the second time around. Maybe in a few days he'd feel differently.

A week, Willy kept thinking. Then he shook his head—he couldn't imagine being stranded for that long. Someone had to figure it out and come after them. It wasn't . . . uh . . . rocket science. Well, it was and it wasn't.

When Willy finished eating, he stood up and gazed out through the branches of the tree. "Are you sure the monsters can't swing like Tarzan?"

"Thortock," Norp said.

"Whatever," Willy said. "Are you sure they can't get to us?"

"The vines won't hold their weight."

Willy nodded. "Lucky for us."

"And lucky that Phelps came along when he did," Cindy said. "That monster didn't know what hit him."

True, the monster—let's call him Sam—didn't have a clue. In fact, it was the first time poop had ever dropped out of the sky and landed in his eyes. He was pretty upset about it, and fairly grossed out. Imagine having poop in *your* eyes. *Eew!*

But that wasn't the worst of it. News of what had happened spread throughout the monster village, which was really just a bunch of caves. Sam, the monster who had been pooped on, was scorned and ridiculed. All of the other monsters laughed and called him names. They wouldn't let poor Sam join in any monster games.

Not only that, but the annual Monster Ball was coming up, and Sam was pretty sure he wouldn't be able to get a date. Would you go out with a guy who'd been pooped on? Didn't think so.

So now he wanted revenge.

If it's the last thing I do, he said to himself.

· · · ·

Willy and his companions had no idea that there was a monster out there who wanted revenge. They knew there were monsters out there, sure. And they knew that they roamed around at night, looking for things to eat. But they had no idea that it was personal.

They had other things to think about, like getting home. "Maybe we should build some kind of signal fire," Willy said.

Cindy scoffed. "A signal fire that can be seen from outer space?"

"Can't be done," Norp added.

"I mean once we see some kind of spaceship, we light a signal fire so they can find us. Someplace where they couldn't miss it, like a mountaintop."

Norp grabbed another piece of fruit from the duffel and took a bite. "Maybe."

"When the sun comes up, we can scout out a good location."

"I love playing with fire," Cindy said.

"Who doesn't?"

While they were discussing where to build the signal fire, and how to build it, and how much fun it would be to play with it once it was built, they heard someone — or some*thing* — cry out in the dark.

"What was that?" Norp asked.

"Not sure," Willy said.

"Sounded like a Tarzan yell," Cindy said.

A few seconds later, they heard what sounded like a human voice. "Knock, knock," the voice said.

Norp put down the fruit he'd been eating. "Did you hear that? Someone just said 'Knock, knock.'"

"I heard it," Willy said. Cindy nodded in agreement.

"Knock, knock," the voice said again.

"There it is again," Norp said with wide eyes. "What do we do?"

Willy shrugged. "Uh . . . who's there?" he called out.

"Oink-oink," came the reply.

Chapter 11

TROUBLE IN THE AMAZON

Things were getting worse in the Amazon jungle.

Willy's father had been the foothunters' prisoner for an entire year. And now they were staring at his feet even more than usual. Every few hours, the foothunter chief and a few of his men walked by the cage where Mr. Maykit was locked up, pointed to his feet, mumbled something in foothunter language, and walked away.

"Something is going on," Mr. Maykit said to himself. He wasn't going to stick around to see what the *something* was. "I've got to get out of here."

That night, he waited until the entire foothunter

village was asleep, then he made his escape . . . or attempted it. The bars of his cage were made of bamboo tied together with thick leather straps. For several minutes he chewed on the straps, but it was no use. They were too thick, and his human teeth were too wimpy.

"Plan B," Mr. Maykit whispered.

But wait a second. Mr. Maykit didn't have a Plan B. He prided himself on coming up with a Plan A that worked every time. Up until now, his Plan A's had always done the job.

Up until now . . .

Now he needed a Plan B, and he needed it quick. There was something scary about the look in the chief's eye. Something *very* scary.

"Plan B," he whispered to himself, looking at the bars of his cage. The leather straps were too tough to chew through. He needed—

It came to him, the perfect Plan B: Get into a

football stance and yell something like, "Twenty-two, sixty-four, hike!" If it was good enough for his college football days, it was good enough for breaking out of a cage in the middle of the Amazon jungle.

Mr. Maykit hit the cage hard — *CRASH!*

It worked. He ran into the jungle, thankful he still had feet to run on.

And run he did. But where to? The Amazon jungle was hundreds of miles in every direction. Mr. Maykit had no idea where to go. For now, he wouldn't worry about that. Put some distance between himself and the foothunters . . . "That's the ticket," he said to himself.

Hours later, when the foothunters woke up to start their day, they were surprised to see their captive had escaped, and even more surprised by *how* he had escaped.

"Darn that American football," the chief said

in foothunter language. Then he sent his warriors after Mr. Maykit. "Don't come back without him."

With any luck, Mr. Maykit had had a good enough head start, and they would never catch up.

With any luck . . .

While Mr. Maykit was running around, lost in a South American jungle, being pursued by foothunters, Willy was on Planet Ed, scratching his head and wondering about the mysterious voice he'd just heard.

"Oink-oink . . . what?" Willy said.

"You're supposed to say, 'Oink-oink who?'" said the voice.

"Oink-oink who?"

"Make up your mind. Are you a pig or an owl?"

Willy looked down. Standing at the base of the tree was Max, the android pilot.

"A pig or an owl," Max said. "Ha, ha . . . that's a real knee slapper. Okay if I come up?"

"Max!" Willy cried. "You came back for us! Can you climb a tree?"

"I can fly a spaceship," Max said. "I'm pretty sure I can climb a tree."

Willy turned around and whispered to Cindy and Norp. "We're saved!" Once again, a band started playing inside him.

Trumpets blared; cymbals crashed. He wanted to break out and dance right there in the tree, a we're-getting-rescued dance, a goodbye-Planet-Ed-hello-Planet-Earth dance, but there wasn't enough room for dancing. Instead, he stepped over his duffel and high-fived Cindy.

"Hooray!" Cindy cheered.

A few seconds later, Max was sitting with them in the tree. "Max, meet Norp," Willy said. "Norp? This is Max."

Max and Norp shook hands.

"Where's the ship?" Cindy asked.

"Yeah, where'd you land?" Willy looked closely at the pilot. Even in the moonlight, he could see that Max's shirt was nearly shredded, his hair singed. There were burn marks on his cheeks, as if sparks had been shooting from his ears. "What happened to you?"

"Yeah," Norp said. "You look like Thortock on a bad day."

"Uh . . ." Max began, "about the ship."

"Yes?" they all said together.

"It's not exactly in working order," Max said.

"What do you mean, not in working order?" Willy said, raising an eyebrow.

"I mean, well . . ." Max hesitated.

"What's wrong with the ship, Max?" Cindy demanded.

"How can I put this?" Max fiddled with his tattered shirt. "It kind of . . . it kind of blew up."

"What?!"

Max started to tell the story, all about how he finally understood the knock-knock joke, and how sparks flew and microchips exploded, and how he couldn't control his arms and legs, let alone the ship, and—

Right in the middle off his explanation, he

spotted Willy's joke book next to the duffel. "You have a joke book?" He crawled over to it and picked it up. "Wow. I love a good laugh."

"Can we get back to what happened to the ship?" Willy said.

Max flipped through the pages of the joke book.

"Max?" Willy said.

Max looked up. "Yes?"

"Finish your story. What happened to the ship?"

Max turned the page. "The ship is no more. I ejected just before it crashed into a mountainside. But listen to this . . . Why can't ghosts tell lies? You can see right through them. Ha, ha! Want to hear another one? How do you get a one-armed baboon out of a tree? Wave! Ha, ha!"

Willy looked at his two companions. "I take that back. Looks like we're *not* rescued after all."

"Now what?" Cindy asked.

"Yeah, what do we do?" Norp said, his antennae beginning to twitch nervously. He glanced up at Max, the tattered android who was busy looking for more jokes to tell and oblivious to everything else.

Willy shook his head. "I have no idea. The ship is destroyed and the pilot has lost his mind."

Chapter 12

PHELPS

Phelps was feeling pretty good about himself. After all, he had saved the lives of three people — or at least two people and an alien, which was something to be proud of. He flew with his head held high. He walked with his chest out. He almost swaggered a few times. And all this confidence caught the attention of a bird, or whatever you call things that fly on Planet Ed.

We'll call her Betty.

Betty flapped down out of the sky and landed on a tree branch next to Phelps and said, "I like a guy with confidence. Want to hang out?" Actually, what she said was "Chirp, chirp, chirp, tweet, chirp," but she meant, "I like a guy with confidence. Want to hang out?"

Phelps turned to her and said, "Absolutely." Actually, what he said was *"Caw,"* but he meant, "Absolutely."

And hang out they did, for most of the day. Then they flew over to a tree occupied by two humans, an alien, and an android with his nose in a book.

By the next morning, Willy, Cindy, and Norp were tired of Max's jokes. They had a signal fire to build, and so they set off early to find a hilltop to build it on.

Max was disappointed. He'd spent all night memorizing every joke in Willy's book, and now there was no one around to tell them to.

No one except Phelps and his new pal Betty. They were sitting on a branch of the tree, watching

Max's every move and looking very much like they wanted to hear something humorous.

Max cleared his throat. Then he looked up at the two birds and said, "What's the difference between a guitar and a fish?"

Phelps tilted his head to one side as if to say, "I don't know. What *is* the difference between a guitar and a fish?"

"You can tune a guitar, but you can't tune a fish." The android smiled. "Isn't that a knee slapper?"

Before Phelps and Betty flew away, he told them another joke, then another. Not all of them were knee slappers, but some of them were. At least Max thought so.

He loved having an audience, even if they were just birds.

Willy and his friends headed through the woods, looking for a place to build a signal fire. As they walked along, Willy began to feel uneasy. Something wasn't right. Norp had said the monsters only came out at night. Still, Willy had the feeling that they were being watched.

"How about there?" Cindy asked, pointing to a clearing. "Nice and flat, with enough room to land a spaceship."

"Looks good to me," Norp said. "Willy?"

Willy kept scanning the trees around them. They were not alone. Something was out there — he was sure of it.

"Willy?" Norp said again.

"Are you sure they only come out at night?" Willy asked.

"Pretty sure," Norp said. Then he pointed to the clearing. "Looks like a good place for a signal fire. What do you think?"

Willy tore his eyes away from the trees and followed his friends. All morning long, they worked on stacking wood for the fire, starting with tiny twigs, then adding larger sticks and logs.

"That's what I call a stack of wood," Cindy said, standing back and gazing at the enormous pile. "We don't light it until we see a ship, right?"

"Right," said Norp.

"How?"

"How what?"

"How do we light it?"

Norp pulled a small box from his pocket. "Don't they have matches on your planet? You can fly through space but you can't light a fire?" He passed out matches to Willy and Cindy. "We can take turns watching the sky. Whoever spots the ship—"

Something went *bump* in the night.

Only it wasn't night, and it didn't go *bump*. It was more like *crack* and *crunch*. Willy's instincts had been correct. Something *was* out there . . . and it was coming their way.

There was more crunching, huge footsteps, branches snapping, and trees bending. And then came the roar—grizzly bear, *T. rex,* and killer whale, all rolled into one.

"I thought you said they didn't come out in the daytime." Willy gasped.

Cindy's knees knocked together like chattering teeth. "Me too."

"I did," Norp said, wide-eyed, "but look!" The monster burst through the trees in front of them and gave another roar. "It's wearing sunglasses."

Sure enough, the monster was wearing sunglasses. And once again it was smiling, an evil, hungry smile. It took a step toward them. Then another . . . and another . . . and then—

Another sound came. Not a monster's roar. This was more like a human voice, some sort of . . . Tarzan yell.

Or a Thortock yell.

Max the android pilot, swinging on a vine, dropped in front of them. Then he took a step toward the monster and said, "Listen up, big fella. A chicken walks into a bar . . ."

Chapter 13

MORE TROUBLE IN THE AMAZON

Even though Mr. Maykit had broken out of the cage that held him by using a football move from his college days, all was not well. He was still lost in a jungle that was hundreds of miles in every direction. And this jungle was one scary place. It had insects as large as his hands, snakes as long as his living room, leopards and panthers and other things with sharp teeth that went *bump* in the night . . . and went *growl* in the daytime. Plus, the weather was blazing hot, and it rained every day.

If the jungle creatures didn't get him, the weather would.

But what scared Mr. Maykit the most were the foothunters who were undoubtedly chasing him. So he kept moving, glancing over his shoulder. The foothunters knew the jungle like the back of their . . . feet. They also had spears and bows and arrows.

Mr. Maykit needed some kind of weapon of his own. He stooped and picked up rocks to throw. He filled his pockets with them. Before becoming an adventurer and scientist, he had been a minor league pitcher. "Have arm, will throw" — that was Mr. Maykit. And he had spent many happy hours teaching his son, Willy, the finer points of throwing a baseball. Slider, knuckle, curve — Mr. Maykit could do it all.

He kept moving, feeling better now that he had rocks to throw. But he needed to find water. Moving water, to be exact. Follow a small creek and you'll find a bigger one. Follow that and you'll eventually find a river. Small rivers lead to larger rivers. Follow a big river long enough and you'll find a village.

Hopefully, not a foothunter village.

That was the plan — he'd find moving water and it would eventually lead him out of the jungle. "I'm coming home, Willy," Mr. Maykit said out loud, thinking of his son. "I'll be home for dinner." Being home for dinner was impossible, and Willy's father knew it. But it kept his spirits up to think this way and made him walk just a little bit faster.

That night, Mr. Maykit climbed a tree and tried to sleep. A tree wasn't the most comfortable place in the world to sleep, but it was better than being on the ground, where all sorts of creepy things lived. Plus, on the ground, the foothunters might stumble upon him in the night.

Sure enough, as Mr. Maykit sat in the tree,

below him the foothunters crept by with their spears, bows and arrows, and blowguns, muttering to one another in foothuner language. Mr. Maykit held his breath until they passed. Then he waited for the sun to rise. When it did, he climbed down and headed in the other direction.

"Find a creek," he said to himself. "Find a river. Find home."

He walked all that day and all the next. But there was no sign of running water. During the daily rainstorms, he collected water from the broad-leafed plants. He ate tiny fruits and other plants to keep his strength up. He was a scientist—he knew which plants were edible and which ones were not.

Then, on the third day, there it was: a small creek, trickling down a hillside. The water was a strange yellowish-brown color, and it called to mind the famous literary work *Yellow River* by I. P. Freely. As far as Mr. Maykit knew, the book was a one-hit wonder. I. P. Freely had never written anything else.

Mr. Maykit smiled. For the first time since breaking out of the foothunters' cage, he was filled with hope. "Follow the creek," he muttered to himself. "That's the ticket."

Chapter 14

RUN!

"Now's our chance," Willy said. "Run!"

The three friends turned and did just that. The monster was occupied, listening to a joke, or at least looking at Max and thinking he'd make a nice mid-morning snack.

In any case, the monster was distracted. It was time to get out of there.

Willy, Cindy, and Norp ran down a slope, stumbling over one another. As they say, you don't have to outrun the beast; you just have to outrun the person next to you.

They kept running, hopping fallen logs, leaping small creeks. Then they sprinted around a bend and—

Right in front of them stood three more monsters, Planet Ed creatures of the night. Only it wasn't dark out at all. It was broad daylight. And they were wearing sunglasses.

"Oh, no! Monsters in sunglasses," Cindy said. "It's a fashion trend!"

A mighty roar. Make that three roars—grizzly bear, *T. rex,* and killer whale, times three.

"Run!"

This time they split up—Norp ran right, Cindy left, and Willy somewhere in between. The monsters split up too—pick a snack, any snack.

Willy tore into the woods, no trail in sight. He blazed his own. Twigs snapped as the monster came after him. Make that branches, not twigs.

Huge branches, now and then a log—*CRACK!* This was no small monster. He was huge and strong. He probably lifted weights in his spare time. He could have his pick of dates to the annual Monster Ball.

Willy ran on until he reached the canyon above the roaring river. On the other side was their tree and safety. He grabbed a vine and swung across, letting out a tiny, victorious Tarzan yell. "Ahh-ee-ahhhh!"

Only he forgot to let go of the vine.

He swung across the canyon. Then he swung back to where the monster was waiting, hands out, ready to grab. Make that claws out.

Willy let go of the vine and down he went. Down, down, down—*KERSPLASH*—into the river. He was swept away, wet, cold, but not a snack. At least not yet.

Once out of the canyon, the river slowed, and Willy pulled himself onto the riverbank. Then he shook himself like a wet dog and looked around. There was no sign of the monster, but also no sign of anything familiar, including Cindy and Norp.

A twig snapped. Then another.

Willy reached down and grabbed some mud from the riverbank. He formed it into a ball and cocked his arm back, ready to throw. He had escaped once before when the monster chasing him was temporarily blinded. But Phelps, the coolest bird in the universe, was nowhere to been seen. How do you blind a monster without bird poop?

Mudball to the eyes — that's how.

"Willy!" Norp popped out of the bushes nearby, holding his hands up. "Don't shoot!"

Willy dropped his arm. "You mean don't throw."

"Whatever."

"Where's Cindy?" Willy asked.

"They got her."

Willy let go of the mudball. "What?" He felt a pang of guilt. If it wasn't for him, Cindy would have been home by now. Instead she was headed for the monsters' breakfast table.

Norp nodded. "What do we do?"

"Ever tracked a monster before?" Willy asked.

"Never. How do we do it?"

Willy sniffed. "Follow the monster breath."

"Guess they don't believe in breath mints on this planet."

"Exactly," Willy said, stooping down to grab another handful of mud from the riverbank. "But first things first. Help me out here, Norp. We need more mudballs."

"Mudballs?"

"They're the only weapon we've got."

Willy and Norp worked quickly, making

mudballs and placing them in the hood of Willy's jacket. Then they set off in search of Cindy.

Fortunately, the monsters had big feet, which meant they left big footprints. There were also broken tree branches and bits of fur left behind. But mostly it was the monster breath that led them. Where you smell monster breath, you find monsters. That's the way it works—nasty breath, nasty monsters.

It wasn't long before Willy and Norp were crouched in the bushes just outside the entrance to an enormous cave.

Willy made a face. "Figures they'd live in a cave."

"What's wrong with that?" Norp asked.

Willy didn't want his alien friend to know that he was absolutely terrified of the dark. At home he slept with a night-light. He glanced at the cave. Something told him there wouldn't be night-lights inside.

"You don't like caves?" Norp asked.

Willy shrugged. "Uh . . . it'll be dark in there. How are we going to find Cindy?"

Norp snorted and pulled a flashlight from his pocket. "What's with you Earthlings? You can travel through space but you don't have flashlights?"

"You're a handy alien to have around," Willy said. He reached into the hood of his jacket and grabbed a few mudballs. "Let's go."

"Yes, let's," Norp said. "But you're the alien."

Being captured by a monster was worse than being picked last in kickball. Worse than being force-fed Brussels sprouts. Worse than being left behind on a faraway planet. Worse than —

Well, let's just say it was worse than a lot of things. This was what Cindy Das was thinking as the monster dragged her deep into the forest and then into an enormous cave.

"Put me down!" she yelled. The monster wasn't listening, and Cindy was about to faint from the smell of monster breath. "Don't you believe in breath mints on this planet?"

Chapter 15

HOW TO KILL A FASHION TREND

Sure enough, there were no night-lights in the monsters' cave. Willy and Norp crept along, monster breath growing fouler by the second.

"Too bad we didn't bring a bunch of breath mints," Norp whispered. "We'd make a killing."

Willy nodded, but he had more important things on his mind. Like rescuing Cindy before the *monsters* made a killing. He just hoped they weren't too late.

Up ahead they saw a flickering light. *Maybe they have night-lights after all,* Willy thought. But as they reached a wide spot in the cave, they found that it was just a fire burning in some type of fire pit—no monsters in sight, and no Cindy. If you think it's strange that monsters know how to build fires, remember this is Planet Ed we're talking about. They not only have monster fires, they have monster games and an annual Monster Ball. On Earth they just live under beds and hang out in closets.

Willy and Norp were about to move on when they spotted a table covered with sunglasses.

"Want to kill a fashion trend?" Willy asked.

"Don't mind if I do," Norp said. He grabbed a handful of sunglasses and tossed them into the fire.

Willy helped until there was nothing left on the table but cave dust.

Then they moved on, and the firelight grew faint. But not the monster breath. Soon they heard noises, low growls and quiet roars.

"Monster talk," Norp whispered.

Willy nodded. "Better turn off the flashlight."

Up ahead they saw more flickering light. It was another fire pit, this time surrounded by monsters, and there was Cindy, still alive. One of the creatures held her by the arm.

"Now what?" Norp whispered.

"I throw, you grab Cindy?"

In the low light of the fire, Willy could see Norp's antennae twitch. "Seriously? That's the plan?"

"You have a better one?" Willy asked. "Besides, you haven't seen me throw. Before my dad became a scientist, he was a minor league pitcher. Taught me how the pros do it."

Norp gave him a strange look. "What's a minor league?" he asked. "What's a pitcher?"

"Baseball," Willy said, as if an alien would understand.

"What?" whispered Norp.

"Never mind."

There was no time to explain America's pastime to a guy from another planet. They had to rescue Cindy before she became breakfast.

"Follow me," Willy said. "I'll create a diversion."

"A what?" Norp whispered.

"A diversion. Mudball diversion. Confuse the monsters while you grab —"

A monster stepped in front of them and let out a huge roar.

"Get Cindy!" Willy yelled as he hurled a mudball.

It was a direct hit, straight to the eyes. Willy threw another one, then another. It was mudball city. Everywhere you looked, flying mud. Monsters

scattered, and in the commotion, the monster holding on to Cindy let go. Norp grabbed her arm, and they both ran deeper into the cave. Willy followed, hurling one last mudball for good measure.

But now what?

They were together again, but inside the enemy's cave, and running away from the entrance. The flying mud had caught the monsters off guard. Soon they'd be giving chase, angrier than ever, ready for a midmorning snack.

There was just one thing to do: run and hope for the best. And so run they did, on and on. One tunnel led to another, which led to another. Meanwhile the growls grew louder behind them.

And then Willy saw something. "I see light," he yelled.

Sure enough, up ahead there was light, and it wasn't flickering like firelight. It was a steady beam coming from—

"Outside," Cindy said, pointing. "There's our escape."

Unfortunately, the hole was too small to crawl

through. It was more of an escape route for a rat . . . or a Chihuahua.

"Dig!" Willy yelled.

Cindy and Norp dug and kicked at the dirt around the hole, making it bigger . . . and bigger. But the Planet Ed creatures were coming up fast.

"Hurry!" Willy yelled.

Finally, Cindy pushed herself through into the daylight, followed by Norp. "Your turn, Willy," he called.

Only now the monsters were upon him. Willy reached into his hood for another mudball. But there was none.

No way out. And no time. Willy needed a plan. What to do when you're all out of mudballs?

Use a spitball instead. Willy reared back and . . . *P-tew.*

Willy was much better at mudballs than

spitballs. The loogey missed by a mile. While he was trying to hock a second attempt, Norp reached through the hole and yanked Willy to safety.

Fresh air at last. Well, not exactly fresh—they could still smell monster breath—but at least they were out of the cave.

Chapter 16
MONSTER BALL

Cindy threw her arms around Willy and Norp. "You guys are the best! Thanks for coming to my rescue."

"Don't mention it," Norp said.

"Yeah," Willy agreed. "All for one, and one for all."

"I could hardly breathe in there," Cindy said. "Monster breath, you know?"

Willy sniffed. "We know." He glanced nervously back at the cave. Any second now, monsters would be pouring out in search of the meal that had eluded them. "We better head back to our tree before they come after us again."

"They can't come after us," Norp said. "We killed their fashion trend, remember?" He turned to Cindy and explained. "We threw all their sunglasses into a fire."

Willy remembered destroying the glasses in the fire, but he also knew that everyone has spare sunglasses. Don't they?

"Spares?" Cindy guessed, reading the scared look on Willy's face.

"Probably," Willy said. "Let's get out of here."

The trio hurried back to the tree, swinging across the canyon like a couple of Tarzans and a Thortock. This time Willy made sure he let go of the vine at the proper time. Soon they were safe and munching a late breakfast of purple fruit.

The monsters never came after them. Maybe they

didn't have spare sunglasses after all. This was what Willy thought. But it was not the case. The monsters had plenty of spares. They had just decided to postpone the hunt for another day. In the meantime, they had their annual Monster Ball to get ready for.

Here's the thing about monsters — they're not very good at making music. Their paws are made for clawing and ripping things apart, not for plucking and strumming fine musical instruments. Still, what's a party without music?

"What's that?" Willy asked from the tree that evening as the sun was going down. Imagine a truckload of musical instruments being dumped onto a field. This was the sound coming from the direction of the monsters' cave — randomly plucked, out-of-tune stringed instruments and blaring horns. No melody at all.

"Sounds like kindergartners broke into a music room," Cindy said, covering her ears.

"Yeah," Norp said. He had no idea what kindergartners were, but he could guess from the look on Cindy's face that they had to be something horrible. "Those monsters could use some music lessons."

The music, or whatever you want to call it, went on for hours, and Willy and his friends could only assume that it was some sort of celebration. What did the monsters have to celebrate, though? That they were mudballed by a fourth-grader? That their breakfast escaped to live another day?

It was a celebration, of course, but it had nothing

to do with Willy, Cindy, and Norp. It was the Monster Ball, the biggest event on the monsters' social calendar. There were monster snacks and monster drinks, monster music and monster dances. And everyone was involved.

Everyone except the one monster who didn't have a date. Everyone except the one monster who'd been pooped on.

And so the monster whom we earlier referred to as Sam didn't attend the Monster Ball. Instead, he wandered away from the party into the forest, looking for revenge, searching for the two humans and the green guy with twitching antennae.

I'll get revenge, he thought. *If it's the last thing I do.*

He wandered about, keeping his eyes peeled and sniffing the air for their scent. Monsters on Planet Ed have a great sense of smell. They also kind of . . . *smell.* Monster breath and monster B.O. is a horrible combination.

Sam climbed a hill and found the pile of wood that Willy and his friends had stacked. *Good time for a marshmallow roast.* He just happened to have the Planet Ed version of marshmallows with him. He lit the fire, grabbed a long stick, and started roasting one after another and popping them into his mouth. He'd much rather have been part of the Monster Ball, but what could he do? He'd been

pooped on and was dateless . . . but boy, did those
marshmallows hit the spot.

. . . .

Willy got up to pee in the middle of the night.

"Where are you going?" Norp asked.

"Nature's calling," Willy told him.

"It is?"

"Don't people pee on your planet?"

"Of course," Norp said. "But what does that have to do with nature calling?"

"Never mind," Willy said, annoyed. "I'll be right back."

Willy climbed down from the tree, and when he did, he saw their signal fire burning in the nearby clearing. He was so upset that he forgot to pee. He quickly climbed back up into the tree.

"Wow," Norp said. "You Earthlings pee fast."

"Someone lit our signal fire!" Willy yelled.

Cindy sat up, rubbing her eyes. "What's going on?"

Willy's face flushed red with anger. "Our signal fire is burning!" He sniffed the air. "I smell marshmallows."

"What do we do?" Norp asked.

Willy shook his head. There was nothing they

could do. It was nighttime, and everyone knew that you didn't go out at night on Planet Ed. Meanwhile, the woodpile that they had worked so hard to stack was slowly turning to ash.

If only we had graham crackers and chocolate, Cindy thought. She'd always loved s'mores.

Chapter 17

WHERE'S MAX?

The next morning they sat in the tree, eating the last of the purple fruit. There was plenty more fruit where those had come from, but now, going out in the daytime was as dangerous as going out at night. The monsters might have spare sunglasses, and if they did, Willy and company would never be safe.

They also no longer had a signal fire.

"What should we do about the signal fire?" Willy asked, wiping juice off his chin. "Build another one?"

"And have someone burn it down again?" Norp asked.

"Exactly," Cindy added. "We stack the wood, and they use it for their weenie roast." It was a marshmallow roast, but you get the idea. Why build something if someone's going to come along and destroy it?

"What's a weenie roast?" Norp asked.

"Never mind," Willy said.

For most of the morning they discussed what to do—build another fire or don't build another fire, gather more of the purple fruit or eat on the run. After a while, Willy's thoughts began to drift. He started thinking of Max. He also thought of Phelps, but mostly it was Max who concerned him. Where was he? What had happened to the joke-telling android?

Max had last been seen swinging on a vine like Tarzan. Or Thortock—take your pick. He had dropped into the clearing, taken a step toward a monster, who, by the way, had very bad breath—Max was an android, but even he could smell it—and then he told a joke about a chicken walking into a bar. Chickens were funny creatures in general. And a chicken going into a bar was hilarious.

This was what Max thought, anyway. Get a monster laughing and he won't want to eat you. But that only works if the monster in question speaks English. The monster in question did not. He was fluent in Monster and only Monster.

When the monster didn't laugh, Max went right into another joke, about a lizard and a doughnut, a real knee slapper. Only the monster didn't get it. He didn't understand. He thought Max looked as delicious as Willy Maykit, and he was way bigger, which meant a larger portion size. The monster came at Max with a mighty roar and took a bite out of his leg.

Max didn't know enough to get out of the way.

He was an android, and androids are machines, and machines don't grow up with monsters living under their beds. In fact, androids don't have beds, so there was no reason to be afraid.

When the monster took a chunk out of his leg, Max wasn't scared. Nor did he feel pain. He was just annoyed. He looked down and saw a hole in his leg. "Hey, stop that!" he yelled. "That's my leg!" It was as if someone had just bumped a shopping cart into a Mercedes. "Hey, look what you did!"

Then Max ran. He didn't run out of fear. It was more like he wanted to protect a fine piece of machinery from some maniac with a sledgehammer.

The problem was that the chunk now missing from his leg

was the part that gave him his sense of direction. He remembered that Willy, Cindy, and Norp's base camp was in a tree on the other side of a deep canyon, but he didn't know how to get there.

Meanwhile, a big hairy guy who didn't understand jokes and preferred large portion sizes was after him.

Max kept running, not realizing that he was getting farther and farther away from Willy and his friends.

Cindy and Norp were in a pretty heated discussion about fire building and fruit gathering. Which was more important, eating or being rescued? Cindy argued in favor of being rescued. For Norp, it was all about food. After all, if you starve to death, who cares if you get rescued? You're already dead.

"But if we get rescued, they'll have food on the

ship." Cindy said. She crossed her arms and glared at Norp.

"Dead people can't eat," Norp said, glaring back.

Willy interrupted. "What do you think happened to Max?" he asked.

This stopped the argument in its tracks. Cindy and Norp turned and looked at Willy.

"What?" Cindy said.

"What?" Norp said.

"Max," Willy said. "Android? Flies spaceships? Tells jokes? Where is he?"

Cindy thought she was getting the upper hand in the build-a-fire/gather-fruit discussion. She hated letting go of a winning argument, but now the thought of Max took over. He was annoying, a little pushy with his joke telling. But hadn't he saved them all when he arrived by vine with a joke? More important, he was part of their group. And now he was missing.

"Max," Cindy said out loud. "He saved our lives. I hope the monster didn't get him."

"What do we do?" Norp said.

"Hmm . . ." Willy said. It had been his idea to introduce humor to the android in the first place. And humor had rescued them—something about a chicken walking into a bar, if he remembered correctly. Humor had also caused Max to crash the ship, but Willy tried not to think about that. "We should go look for him."

"It's a pretty big planet out there," Cindy said. "Where do we begin?"

This started another discussion on the dangers of wandering away from the safety of their tree, now that the monsters were out and about day *and* night. On the other hand, at some point they'd need food and water. They'd have to risk it.

"Yep, food and water," Norp said, smiling

victoriously at Cindy. He gave himself a pat on the back. The food argument was winning.

Cindy ignored Norp and decided not to argue. Eat, drink, and get rescued. That would work. "No time like the present. Let's go. Willy, grab the duffel."

Willy slung his father's duffel over his shoulder and climbed down from the tree. Then he pushed through the circle of trees and stopped. There on the ground was a huge pile of—

"Monster poop!"

Norp squeezed between the trees, followed by Cindy. "What?" they said in unison.

Willy pointed to the ground, then glanced nervously at the forest around them. "How do you think they got across the canyon?"

"Not sure," Norp said. "Maybe they can swing on vines after all."

"Let's get out of here," Cindy said. "Our safe tree is no longer safe."

Willy and Norp nodded. They swung across the canyon and headed into the forest, glancing nervously around them. They knew they wouldn't be coming back to the tree.

Planet Ed was becoming more dangerous by the second.

Chapter 18

A NEW HOME

They moved through the forest, each with his or her own agenda. Willy wanted to find Max, Norp wanted food, and Cindy was torn between creating a rescue plan and finding new shelter. They kept walking, scanning the trees around them, keeping their eyes peeled . . . and their noses perked. They could smell monster breath a mile away. Maybe having no breath mints was a *good* thing.

Cindy stopped suddenly. She turned to Willy and Norp. "What about the wreckage of the Starlite?"

Norp cocked an eyebrow. "Starlite?"

"The spaceship," Willy explained. He turned to Cindy. "What about it?"

"There's got to be something left of it," Cindy said. "Fuselage, galley, computer parts. I bet we could rig something up and send a distress signal. Way better than a signal fire."

"Did you say something about a galley?" Norp asked, licking his lips.

Cindy turned to him and nodded. "I bet you there's even food."

"I'm in." Norp was getting excited. "Lead the way."

"And if enough of the ship is still intact, we have a new home base," Willy said.

"Exactly," Cindy said. "Maybe with locking doors. Those monsters are strong, but they're not that strong."

The problem was how to find the downed Starlite. They had no idea where to look. And Planet Ed was huge.

"Remember the night we heard that big explosion?" Cindy asked. "I said I hoped the monsters didn't have dynamite. It wasn't dynamite. It was the ship crashing."

"You're right," Willy said, pointing. "And it came from that direction. Follow me." He headed off into the trees, blazing a new trail. "A new hide-out — cool."

"Rescue," Cindy said.

"Food," Norp added.

Three agendas, one journey. Willy kept walking, leading the way. Overhead, dark clouds began to gather. Now and then they heard a thunderclap off in the distance. So far there was no rain.

For most of the morning, the trio walked in silence. On the night of the crash, the explosion had seemed fairly close to their tree hideout, but there was no sign of a wrecked ship.

"Didn't Max say the ship crashed into the side of a mountain?" Norp asked. "Maybe we need to find higher ground."

They were standing beneath a large pine tree . . . or the Planet Ed version of pine. Willy glanced at the branches above them. "I'll go up and take a look around." After all, he was an explorer. Looking around was what he did best. Seeing what was lurking around the bend was in his blood. Hopefully, he could spot the downed Starlite.

Willy climbed the tree.

"Well?" Cindy yelled to him after a while.

"Hold on," Willy said. He kept climbing. "A little higher." He stopped and scanned the forest around him, to the right, then to the left. "I think I see some—"

Willy's foot slipped and he fell, straddling the branch he'd been standing on.

"Ouch," Norp said, wincing. "I hate when that happens."

"Are you okay, Willy?" Cindy called up to him.

Willy tried to nod, but he didn't want to lie. He

climbed back down. "Oh, my aching you-know-what," he said in a high voice.

"I know what," Norp said, wincing again.

"I don't know what," Cindy said. She turned to Willy. "*What?*"

"Never mind," Willy said. "I think I saw something. It's to the right, on the side of a hill. Looked like something metal hidden among the trees."

"Sounds promising," Cindy said.

"Yes, lead on," Norp said. Where there was metal hidden among the trees, there could be a crashed spaceship. And where there was a crashed spaceship . . . Norp licked his lips again, thinking of the possibilities. "Let's hurry."

They moved on, Willy once again leading the way. He was a little sore from his fall. Still, the excitement of finding what was left of the Starlite kept him going. Meanwhile, thunder continued to roar off in the distance. So far, it hadn't started to rain, but the sky was growing darker by the second.

They kept hiking up the side of the hill. But there was no sign of a wrecked anything, let alone a wrecked spaceship. Willy decided to climb another tree and take another look around. This time he didn't climb as high and was careful not to slip.

"Well?" Cindy asked when he reached the ground.

"Something's there," he said with a smile. "We're close."

An hour later, they were walking among the wreckage of the Starlite. "Not much left," Willy said, disgusted, kicking at the debris. He had really hoped they'd find enough of the ship for a new home base. All about them lay blackened pieces of metal and the remains of electronic parts. Half of the cockpit's control panel hung from a tree. Shattered

glass crunched beneath their feet. "Good thing Max ejected."

"There's gotta be something we can use," Cindy said. "Keep looking."

"Where's the galley?" Norp looked the saddest of the three. The thought of food had kept him moving as they hiked the steep hillside to the wreckage. But there was no sign of anything edible, just a burned-out crash site.

And then—

"Look!" Cindy yelled, pointing through the trees. Fifty yards away, there was more of the Starlite. "The ship must have split in two. This is just the front half." She hurried through the forest to the rest of the wreckage, followed by Willy and Norp. There were bits of tables and parts of couches. A large chunk of the movie screen dangled from a fallen tree. Three metal toilets lay in a row. And the library was fully intact . . . or mostly so.

Cindy tried the door and swung it open. Inside, smashed computer monitors were strewn about. Cindy and Willy picked through the rubble, while Norp moaned about there being no food.

"If we send out a distress call, someone will come to our rescue," Cindy told him.

"Someone with food," Willy added.

"Good point," Norp said, joining in the search for something usable. "I'm great with computers. I'm better at eating, but I know computers."

"Me too," Cindy said.

"Not me," Willy said. "I'm an explorer, not a computer geek."

Norp straightened up and pointed toward the door. "Okay, Willy, you go find us something to eat. Cindy and I will work on sending out a distress call."

"I'm on it," Willy said. He headed out and down the hillside. Far away, in the valley below, he could see a grove of pink trees. Where you find pink trees, you find purple fruit. He'd prefer a cheeseburger, but purple fruit would do in a pinch.

Chapter 19

SOMETHING SMELLS FISHY

What is it about aliens and food? Willy thought as he walked along. Hadn't they just eaten breakfast? Still, if they could get a distress call going, he was glad to do his part by making Norp happy. As they say, the way to an alien's heart is through his stomach.

Willy kept walking. After some time, he came across a small creek and decided to follow it. It was heading downhill, as creeks do. And downhill was where the pink trees were. Food and water right in the same place. Not bad.

Something flashed in the water. Willy stopped and stared. There it was again—a silver flash,

161

not one, but many. Planet Ed had fish? A hot dinner would really hit the spot. Norp would be one happy alien. But how do you catch a fish without a rod and reel? Willy glanced around at the smooth, skinny branches of a nearby tree. With a spear, that's how.

Overhead, thunder roared, or maybe it clapped. The point is that a whole lot of noise was coming from the clouds. And it was much closer this time. Willy felt a few drops of rain. He didn't care. Rain or no rain, he was going to catch a fish.

He broke a thin branch off the tree, about the thickness of his finger, and got to work sharpening the tip on the rough surface of a boulder.

The wind began to pick up. Then —

CRACK!

Lightning flashed.

"Lightning, schmightning," Willy muttered. "Just don't scare my fish."

The rain began to pick up and so did the wind as he crept to the edge of the pool where he had seen the fish. Willy cocked his arm back. He could hit anything with a baseball. How difficult could it be to hit a fish? After all, the fish were much closer than a fellow player on a baseball field.

"Here goes," Willy whispered. He jabbed the spear, and—

A direct miss.

He tried a second time, correcting his aim.

Again he missed.

Third time's a charm? Not even close. The fourth wasn't any better, nor was the fifth.

By this time the fish were so spooked that he had to move downstream to find another pool with an unsuspecting fish . . . or three. A few minutes later, Willy found another pool. He cocked his arm back, and—

"Yes!" he yelled, pumping a fist. He hit a fish dead-center. *Hot dinner, coming right up.* Willy was so excited, he went after another fish. Then another.

Even as lightning cracked and thunder roared, even as the rain came down harder, along with a fierce wind, Willy couldn't help smiling. He'd caught three fish on a faraway planet, in a faraway solar system. And he did it without a rod and reel. "This is what you call a good day," he said out loud.

Right then, a monster stepped out of the woods and gave a tremendous roar.

"This is what you call a *bad* day!" Willy screamed. He ran. Little did he know that the monster in question just happened to hate his guts. Being chased by a monster was bad enough. Being chased by one with a grudge was way worse.

The storm surged.

CRACK! Lightning struck.

And then—*CRACK!*—trees started dropping their body parts, all while Willy was being pursued by a huge, hairy guy with an attitude. Make that a huge, *wet,* hairy guy with an attitude. A wet dog smells pretty nasty. Try a wet monster. *Eew!* If the claws didn't get him, the bad smell would.

Willy kept running—*CRACK!*—avoiding falling

tree branches — *CRACK!* — and taking his chances with the lightning strikes.

Meanwhile, the monster gained, growling horribly. He'd been pooped on by a seagull, shunned by his own kind, and he'd missed the annual Monster Ball. This was one angry beast.

And then —

CRACK! It was the lightning strike to beat all lightning strikes. The impact threw Willy to the ground. He turned just in time to see a large tree fall right on top of you-know-who. Then came a roar that was not grizzly bear crossed with *T. rex*. It had no hint of killer whale. It was more like a moose with a charley horse or a cow with a toothache, low and miserable and full of pain.

The monster's legs were trapped beneath the tree. He looked up at Willy with eyes no longer filled with rage, and moaned again.

"Let that be a lesson to you, big guy," Willy said, getting to his feet. Then he walked away.

"It was an act of nature," Willy said to himself as he returned to the creek to grab his duffel. The fish he'd caught were inside. "All's fair in love and monster fighting. He was trying to get me and a tree fell. It's not my fault."

His arguments made sense. After all, it *was* an act of nature, and it *wasn't* really his fault. But then why couldn't he get the monster's moan out of his head? Why couldn't he shake off the look he'd seen in the monster's eyes?

Ten minutes later, Willy was standing in front of the monster. "Do you know what a good deed is, big guy? It's kind of like this: If I was to help get this tree off you, that would be a good deed. Do you understand?"

The monster just stared at him and moaned.

"And if someone does you a good deed, you shouldn't eat him. That's how it works where I come from."

More moaning from the monster.

"I'm just saying," Willy continued, "I'm thinking of helping you out here. And you should be nice when I do. Okay?" If only they taught monster language in school. Willy could say a few things in Spanish, but that was about it. "So the deal is, I help you, and you keep your teeth to yourself. *Comprendes?*"

More moaning from the monster, but no indication that it understood English *or* Spanish.

Willy got to work, hoping his kindness wouldn't backfire. He grabbed a long piece of wood, about as thick as his thigh, and stuffed the tip under the fallen tree. Next he found another log to use as a fulcrum. This was third-grade science stuff. Willy knew all about moving heavy objects with levers.

"Okay, here goes!" he yelled. "All you need is some wiggle room."

Willy threw all of his weight on the other end of the lever. Very slowly the log began to rise. Not much, but it was enough for the monster to pull free. He stood up and looked at Willy.

"Easy," Willy said, holding his palms out. "We had an agreement, right?"

The monster threw his head back and roared. Then he limped away into the forest.

Chapter 20
PHONE HOME

Willy grabbed the duffel with the fish inside and headed up the hill toward the wrecked Starlite. He didn't have any of the purple fruit, but he had something better: the makings of a hot dinner. Would Norp eat fish? Probably. Norp was an eating machine.

As he trudged uphill, Willy kept turning around, scanning the forest behind him for any sign of the monster with a limp. Maybe getting hit by a tree had given him some kind of short-term memory loss and he'd already forgotten about Willy's good deed. Or maybe his legs were too sore to give chase then, but they felt better now. All these thoughts filled Willy's head. What if he was being stalked this very second? He stood still and listened. Nothing but the wind in the trees, now that the rain had stopped. He sniffed. Nothing but the Planet Ed version of pine needles.

No monster in the area, Willy concluded. He moved on. When he reached the crash site, he tossed the duffel on the ground in front of the door to the library.

"Food!" Norp came out, smacking his lips. He stooped and unzipped the duffel. "What the —" He was expecting purple fruit, not dead fish.

Willy bent down and grabbed one of the fish, which was fifteen inches long, maybe more. "How do we clean it?"

Norp snorted as he reached into his pocket and pulled out a pocketknife. "What is it with you Earthlings?" he said, opening the 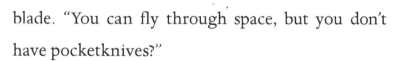 blade. "You can fly through space, but you don't have pocketknives?"

"Do you know how to clean it?" Willy asked.

"If it's food, I'll do what I have to."

Fair enough, Willy thought, happy that someone else would be doing the fish cleaning. *Catching* the fish had been fun. Cleaning it? Not so much.

Cindy stepped out of the library. "Fish?" she said.

"Hot dinner," Willy said. "How'd it go here? Were you able to send a distress signal?"

"Let me show you," Cindy said. "You're gonna love it."

Willy put the fish back inside the duffel and handed the bag to Norp. "Have at it," he told him.

Norp nodded and dragged the duffel to the edge of the trees and got to work. Meanwhile, Willy followed Cindy inside the library. "Wow," he said. The entire room had been cleaned. All broken monitors had been removed and the floor swept of broken glass.

Cindy pointed to a monitor with a blinking message:

Party of three stranded on Ed. Need rescue.

"Every five seconds we blast the message out into space," Cindy said proudly.

Willy looked confused. "But how?"

"We hooked it up to a satellite dish outside, using

a bunch of laptop batteries for power. Norp figured it out. He makes the computer geeks on Earth seem like kindergartners."

And he knew how to clean fish. Willy was liking their alien friend more and more.

"But wait a second," Willy said, staring at the monitor. "Ed is *our* name for the planet. So only Earth ships will understand it."

"We thought of that too," Cindy said. A few feet away, there was another monitor set up, flashing a different message:

Party of three stranded on Preak. Need rescue.

"Preak?" Willy said. "That's what they call it on Norp's planet?"

"Named after some guy's dog," Cindy explained. "Or their version of a dog. But I haven't shown you the best part." She grabbed Willy by the arm and dragged him to the far end of the room. "We found the movie projector and got it working."

"Powered by more laptop batteries?" Willy asked.

"Uh-huh." Cindy grinned. "Want to watch a movie tonight?"

"Sure."

And so, that evening, after roasting their fish over an open fire, where Willy recounted his adventures of catching the fish and doing a good deed for a monster who wanted to eat him, they retreated to

the library and watched a movie . . . or two, which they projected onto the side of the ship.

Their bellies were full, and they had movies to watch. Not a bad way to spend an evening if you're stranded on a faraway planet in a faraway solar system.

"If only we had popcorn," Cindy complained.

"What?" Norp asked.

"Never mind."

While the movie-watching and popcorn-craving was going on, Max, who had been wandering around for some time, found his way back to the tree across the canyon by pure luck. Only it was a deserted tree—with a pile of monster poop at the base.

"Anybody home?" Max called out.

No answer.

Except . . . "*Caw.*"

Phelps and his new pal Betty had also found their way back to the tree.

But Willy, Cindy, and Norp were nowhere to be seen.

"Where is everybody?" Max asked the bird.

"Caw." That was all Phelps had to say on the matter. In fact, it was all he had to say on *any* matter.

Max didn't bother climbing. Instead, he swung across the canyon on a vine and headed into the trees in search of his friends. Overhead, Phelps and Betty followed.

Chapter 21

ONE GOOD DEED . . .

The next morning, Norp woke with one word on his mind. "Food!"

"Good morning to you, too," Cindy said, yawning.

Willy and Cindy were hungry as well, but Norp craved food like it was going out of style.

"I know where there's a grove of pink trees," Willy said. "Maybe we should stick together this time."

"So the monsters will have their choice of who to eat?" Norp asked.

"Something like that," Willy said. "I'd feel safer if we were all together."

Cindy and Norp agreed. Now that the distress signals were being sent, sticking together was the plan. They started down the hillside, Willy leading the way. Soon they reached the creek where Willy had caught the fish. There were plenty more where they had come from, but for now, purple fruit was on the menu.

It was still a little damp from the rainstorm. Steam rose off the soggy ground. They were in for a hot and muggy day. If the monsters were out, they'd need sunglasses. The question was, did they have spares?

In any case, Willy again felt like they were being watched. He nervously scanned the trees around them. He sniffed the air for any sign of—

"Monster breath!" Willy yelled suddenly.

"I smell it too," Cindy said. And she should

know. Of the three, she'd spent the most time in their foul-smelling cave.

And then —

Monster roars, one after another. Moments later, Willy and company saw movement in the forest. Multiple roars meant multiple monsters. All of them hungry. All of them wearing sunglasses.

"Guess we didn't kill that fashion trend after all," said Norp.

Cindy's knees began to knock.

"Run!" Willy yelled.

Down the hillside they ran, snarling, growling monsters hot on their heels, gaining with every step. Tremendous roars sounded all around them — grizzly bear, *T. rex,* and killer whale, times twenty.

It was an all-out sprint down the hill. Willy leaped a fallen log and kept going. Cindy dove across a creek, rolled, and was back on her feet. Norp ran faster than he'd ever run in his life. But it wasn't enough.

The monsters were gaining, growling and snapping their sharp monster teeth.

Then another roar sounded, the biggest one of all, grizzly bear, *T. rex,* and killer whale, with a hint of . . . Harley Davidson motorcycle?

"Don't like the sound of that," Willy muttered. Did these monsters have an older brother who had just joined the chase?

"Me neither," Norp said, picking up the pace.

Willy shuddered at the thought of another monster bigger than the ones he'd already seen. Bigger, hairier, hungrier — and with nastier monster breath.

"Faster!" yelled Norp.

"Spaceship!" Cindy yelled, pointing to the sky.

The gigantic roar was an engine roar, not a bigger version of monster. Their rescue had arrived at last!

Only it was too late. Willy, who was looking up at the ship, tripped and fell to the ground. Cindy tumbled over him, followed by Norp. The monsters closed in, jaws snapping, claws out.

"I'm too young to die," Willy squeaked.

"Me too," Cindy said.

"I haven't even had breakfast," Norp complained.

The monsters kept moving forward, slowly now, savoring their kill.

Willy tried to get back to his feet, but he was too scared to move. He glanced over at his friends. "Been nice knowing you."

"You too," Norp said.

Cindy nodded but said nothing.

But then a monster limped out of the forest to their right and stood between Willy and his friends and the approaching band of monsters.

Willy would know that limp anywhere. "Thanks, big guy." He jumped to his feet, dragging Cindy and Norp along with him. "Let's go."

They ran down the hill and into a clearing, where a small spaceship was waiting. It wasn't a Starlite 3000, but Willy didn't care. A spaceship was a spaceship. A rescue was a rescue.

Willy and his friends raced for the ship. Behind

them, the monsters were coming up fast. The monster with a limp had stalled them temporarily. Now the chase was on again.

This time Cindy took the lead, followed by Norp and Willy.

"That's not the Starlite!" Cindy yelled.

"Who cares?" Willy said. "Look what's behind us."

"Good point," Cindy said.

The final fifty yards was an all-out sprint, monsters gaining at every step, jaws snapping, monster breath smelling nastier than ever.

And then Cindy tripped, which sent Norp sprawling. But not Willy. He leaped over them both and yanked them to their feet. "Almost there," he said.

Willy, Cindy, and Norp dove for the opening of the ship just as the closest monster lunged.

And missed.

The door slid shut, and the ship rose slowly into the air.

High-fives all around. They were safe at last.

And then—

"Wait!" Cindy yelled, pointing out the window. "It's Max."

Sure enough it *was* Max. He burst out of the trees from the other side of the clearing. Overhead flew Phelps and another bird, heading for the ship.

"We can't leave without them," Willy said. "Put this thing back down."

Willy watched in horror as the monsters turned toward Max.

"Run, Max," Cindy said under her breath.

Overhead the two birds dive-bombed.

Glop!

Glop!

It was a double whammy. Their aim was perfect.

"Put this thing down!" Willy yelled again.

The ship landed once more and opened the door, but only long enough for Max and the two birds to get on board. Then it lifted off again, leaving Planet Ed and some very disappointed monsters behind.

Chapter 22

HOME AGAIN

Willy glanced over at Norp, breathing hard. He smiled and said, "You're going to love our planet."

Norp gave him a confused look. "What?"

The cockpit door slid open, and out stepped one of the pilots. He was an older version of Norp: green skin, with two antennae sticking out of his head.

"*You're* going to love *my* planet," Norp said.

Willy glanced over at Cindy, then out the window. Beneath them, the clearing was filling up with Planet Ed creatures of the night, all wearing sunglasses and looking up at the ship.

Once again Willy found himself heading to a

new planet. He had no idea what to expect, and the thought scared him.

They were headed *away* from Earth, not toward it. How was he going to get home?

"What do we do?" Cindy whispered, eyeing the pilot.

Willy shook his head. "Not sure," he whispered back. If only he could convince the aliens to drop him, Cindy, and the others off before heading to their home planet. He scratched his head and thought it over. How could he convince them? How could he entice them to—

Willy had an idea. He turned to Norp and said, "It's too bad we're not going to our planet. We have the best food in the universe."

Norp, who had been staring out the window, turned and looked at Willy. "What was that?"

"Yep." Willy let out a sigh. "The best food in the entire universe. Especially this one food. We call it—" He thought of his favorite things to eat: hot fudge sundaes, root beer floats, cheeseburgers, pizza. But which one would appeal to an alien? "We call it . . . uh—"

"Waffles," Cindy said.

Willy turned to her. *Hmm, not bad.* "Waffles," he agreed.

Cindy went on. "They're made by this special machine.

And you can put all kinds of toppings on them. Maple syrup, strawberries."

"Whipped cream," Willy added.

Norp licked his lips. "Waffles? Really? What do they taste like?"

"They're to die for," Willy said, glancing at Cindy for confirmation.

"Uh-huh," Cindy said, nodding. "To die for."

Willy let out another sigh. "Too bad, though. We're heading in the wrong direction."

The pilot said, "Best food in the universe? Really?"

"Really," Willy said.

"Absolutely," Cindy said. "Waffles. You gotta try them."

The door to the cockpit slid open again, and out stepped the other pilot. "What's this about food?" Obviously, the ship was on autopilot. No need to steer when you're traveling along at many times the speed of light.

"Which way to your planet?" asked the first pilot.

The other pilot nodded and licked his lips. "Yes, how do we get there?"

"Turn left at Pluto?" Cindy suggested in a small voice.

"Turn left at Saturn," Willy said. Saturn was bigger than Pluto. Plus, it had rings. It might be easier to find. Then again, the universe was a very big place. Maybe there were plenty of planets that looked exactly like Saturn. Willy didn't know. But

he didn't want the pilots to know he didn't know. "Yep, turn left at Saturn," he said with confidence. "Isn't that right, Cindy?"

"Yes. Turn left at Saturn," she said. "That'll get us there. I can almost smell those waffles already."

It was a six-hour trip back to Earth, mostly because it took so long to find Saturn. Once they did, they found Jupiter, then Mars, and . . .

"That's Earth there," Willy said, pointing to the alien computer screen in the cockpit. There was something very wrong about a fourth-grader being in the cockpit of an alien spaceship, but if it was okay with these waffle-loving aliens, it was okay with Willy Maykit.

When they reached Earth, they dropped Cindy off first. It was nighttime when the ship touched down in her backyard.

"Thanks for coming after me," Willy told her as she stepped off the ship. "I'll never forget it."

She smiled. "Of course. See you at school, Willy." Then she turned to Norp. "You're the nicest alien I know, Norp. Safe travels."

"Thanks," Norp said. "But you're the alien."

Max, who had the joke book tucked under his arm, got out too. So did the two birds.

"Caw," said Phelps as he took to the air, which was probably his way of saying, "Planet Ed is a nice place to visit, but I wouldn't want to live there."

The spaceship lifted off the ground and flew across town to Willy's house. "Wait here," Willy said to Norp and the two pilots. "I'll only be a second." Then he ran up the back porch steps and into the house. "Mom!" he yelled. "I'm home."

Mrs. Maykit, who was in her room getting ready for bed, came into the kitchen. "Willy!" she screamed, scooping him up in her arms. "I can't believe it. But how on earth—"

"Got any waffle mix, Mom?" he asked.

"Of course. You must be starving," Mrs. Maykit said.

"Not for me," Willy said. He went to the door and, putting two fingers in his mouth, whistled. "Don't freak when you see my friends, Mom. They gave me a ride home, and I promised to feed them."

"Waffles?" she asked.

"Waffles," Willy said. "But seriously, don't freak."

Mrs. Maykit *did* freak, but only a little. For the most part, she was the perfect host. So what if her guests had green skin? So what if they had antennae sticking out of their heads? So what if they ate three times as much as any human could eat? She was just happy to have her son home again.

"Wow," said one of the pilots, reaching for the syrup. "You were right. This really is the best food in the universe."

"Told ya," Willy said.

When the meal was over, Norp walked up to Willy and shook his hand. "You're the nicest alien I've ever met," he said.

"Thanks," Willy said. "But you're the alien."

They both laughed.

"Great to meet you," Willy told him.

"Likewise," Norp said.

A few minutes later, the alien ship lifted off the ground while Willy and his mom waved from the back porch.

"You make a mean waffle, Mom," Willy said.

"Thanks, Willy." They went back inside. "And that must have been some adventure you had."

"Adventure? What adventure?" said a voice.

Standing in the doorway to the living room was Mr. Maykit, clothes in tatters, in dire need of a shave, and with a lifetime's worth of bug bites. He was smiling.

"Dad!" Willy yelled, running to him.

It was the tearful reunion to beat all tearful reunions. Willy and his parents cried buckets of tears. They cried rivers. They could have gone outside and watered the lawn, but no one cared about watering anything. The Maykits were back together again, and that was all that mattered.

Through the tears and between hugs, Mr. Maykit told the story of how he had been captured by foothunters, how he escaped, and how he found his way out of the jungle by following a river system.

Then he said to Willy, "What about your adventure?" Mr. Maykit was a bigtime scientist and an even bigger-time adventurer. If his son had a story to tell, Mr. Maykit wanted to hear it.

While Mrs. Maykit cooked up another waffle . . . or three, Willy sat at the table with his father and told his own story. "It was a class field trip to Planet Ed. I saw a trail leading into the woods, and I had to see what was beyond the bend, didn't I?"

"Of course," said Mr. Maykit, ruffling Willy's hair. "Absolutely."

Willy told him everything: about being left behind, about Cindy and Norp, and hailstorms, and monsters, and Max, and jokes, and purple fruit, and Tarzan yells —

Willy looked at his father's tattered clothes and overgrown beard. "You know something, Dad? You look like Thortock on a bad day."

"Thortock?"

"He's an alien version of Tarzan," Willy told him.

"I'll take that as a compliment."

Mrs. Maykit came in from the kitchen and placed a plate of waffles on the table. Then she sat down with her family.

"It's good to be home," Mr. Maykit said.

"Yes," Willy agreed, reaching for his parents' hands. "I really missed you guys."

GREG TRINE has never traveled outside the solar system, but it's on his to-do list. In the meantime, he writes books. His other titles for kids include the Adventures of Jo Schmo series and the Melvin Beederman, Superhero series. Greg lives with his family in California. Visit him at www.gregtrine.com.

JAMES BURKS spends a lot of time in space dreaming of creatures and galaxies far, far away. While on Earth, he creates books for kids such as his Bird and Squirrel graphic novel series. He lives with his family in California. Visit him at www.jamesburks.com.